Audition for Death

A Joshua Mclintock Mystery

by

Steve Shrott

Copyright © 2013 by Steve Shrott

For information, email **Cozy Cat Press**,

cozycatpress@aol.com or visit our website at:

www.cozycatpress.com

COZY CAT
PRESS

ISBN: 978-1-939816-26-9

Printed in the United States of America

Cover design by Laura Redmond

http://lauradawnsky.info

1 2 3 4 5 6 7 8 9 10

I'd like to send my appreciation to Patricia Rockwell for believing in this book. I'd also like to thank my mom and dad for being wonderful parents and especially my brother, Barry, for always being there for me in every way possible.

Chapter One

Everything was going smoothly in my life—made a few sales, won a couple of bucks at the track, met a sweet lady or two. Then last Thursday, my life got twisted around like two pretzels doing the wild thing.

The name's Mclintock—Joshua Mclintock. I'm an actor. Heard of me? Okay, I'm not a household name--yet. I know what you're thinking, in L.A. everyone's an actor. Right on; my plumber is up for the same roles I am. The sad part is a lot of times he gets them.

When I'm not acting, I work at LLG Productions. It's located in beautiful Leaside, California, home of street gangs and car jackings. Although I'm not sure that's their motto.

I'm one of those guys who upsets your dinner by trying to get you to buy magazines on the phone. You know the major ones like 'Time,' 'People,' and 'Sports Illustrated.' Great magazines, at a low price, right to your door, every month. Only $59.99 plus...sorry, didn't mean to give you the spiel but I get carried away sometimes.

I skulked in late, trying to avoid the boss's lecture about how we should be punctual and all that malarkey, when I felt a steel finger boring its way into my trapezius.

"Mr. Mclintock..."

I whirled around to face Walter Lowenthal, our beloved commander in chief. He certainly hadn't gotten any better looking since the last time I'd seen him. His skin was still as pale as paste and he had a nose that looked like it had gone two rounds with a brick wall. One thing you had to say for him is that he never had a hair out of place. Of course, when you only had two, I guess that isn't a big deal.

"Yes, sir." I said. We had to call him 'sir,' do you believe it? The next think you know we'll all be bowing and kissing his ring.

"You're late."

"Yeah, well, I had this audition at eight in the morning."

"What you do outside of this office is of no concern––"

"It was Shakespeare."

"–to me."

"Hamlet."

"This is the second time, Mclintock." He prodded me again with that damn finger.

"It went very well, thanks for asking."

"Ahh." He tossed his hand toward me as if to say, 'buzz off,' then, shaking his head, he headed to his office. Oh, I know I talk back to him, but he can't fire me. Jeez, I make him more money than any two telephone guys put together. But I'm not interested in making this my career or anything like that. It's just something to do between roles. The depressing part is that lately there's been a whole lot of 'between.'

The morning started off pretty slow so I had lots of time to talk to my fellow workers—Frank, Abe, Sherry and Keenan. Frank is a hell of a nice guy, works here part time. His real job is being a clown for kids' birthday parties. Makes pretty good dough.

And when I first spoke to Sherry, I thought she was the sweetest woman I'd ever met. Then I found out that 'she' was a 'he' and that changed my thinking on the matter. I still think he's sweet; I'm just not sure I want to ask him out anymore.

It turned out to be a good day. By noon, I'd gotten three suck...I mean 'respected and valued' clients to order a years worth of *The Economist*. I work differently than most of the telemarketers I know. Most phone guys just call everyone on their lead lists. But a name has to do something to me before I get on the blower. That's what gives me the edge. My first victim was Mary Waterson. I felt the good vibes bouncing right off ol' Mare, so I picked up the phone and dialed.

"Hello, Miss Waterson?"

"Yes?" What a voice, I was in love already.

"It's Joshua Mclintock calling from..."

"Is this about dance lessons?"

"Oh, no."

"Furnace cleaning?"

"Not at all."

"Magazines?"

"Well, uh..." Click. Guess the vibes weren't as good as I thought. The best thing to do after a bad call is to get back on that horse. I found another name that hit me right in the cajonies. I dialed. "Hello. Is Mr. Wallace Greg there?"

"This is Greg."

"How are you on this fine spring morning?"

"Okay."

"Today, Mr. Greg, we're offering a free subscription to Time magazine. How does that sound?"

"Terrific."

"Well, of course, you have to qualify first."

"Oh?" His voice was a mixture of anticipation and puzzlement. I'd struck pay dirt.

"Just a few short questions. Do you own your own home?"

"Yeah."

"Do you earn $10 to 20,000, 20,000 to 40,000 or over 50,000 a year?"

"Twenty to forty."

"Great. Now to get your free subscription to *Time,* all you have to do is order a year's subscription to *People* or *Sports Illustrated.* Isn't that easy?"

I waited for his response but didn't hear any. Suddenly, there was a fire-cracker sound and a loud thump.

"I've been shot."

Chapter Two

The phone went dead. I quickly dialed the number again, but all I got was a busy signal. What had happened? Was he still alive? I thought about what to do when a phone book whizzed by my head, and sent several pieces of plaster flying from the wall. Lowenthal stepped in front of me holding his stopwatch.

"Mclintock, you were on that call three minutes too long. That's going to come out of your break."

"Three minutes is my break."

"C'est la vie."

"That man was shot."

"Shot? You mean with a gun?"

I nodded.

"You hitting the sauce again, Mclintock?"

"Don't keep throwing that in my face man, I've been dry for six months." I was about to make his bent nose, even more bent, but luckily, I came to my senses. "Look, I gotta phone the cops about this."

"Your job is sales not crime reporting, kapesh?"

"Yeah, right. Just let me handle it my way." Then I gave him my maniac look, the one I used in the movie, *The Stingy Strangler*. I think it scared him.

"As you wish," he grunted.

I sat down and waited till he was back in his office before I made the call. As I lifted the receiver, I noticed my hand shaking. Not that I'm nelly nervous, but it's not everyday someone buys the farm while you're talking to him about a magazine subscription. Anyway,

I spoke to a sergeant at 32 Division, who took my name and said he'd look into it. But he told me it might take a while to get back to me cause they had a lot on their plate right now.

I had a lot on my plate too. I had to get to the Roncenville Theatre for the eight o'clock curtain call. I had been appearing nightly as the servant in the play, *Dirty Old Men*. I made it to the theatre without a second to spare. Tonight was the last performance and I gave my lines an extra special zing. I was actually only on stage for 7.3 seconds, but I believe that's what rallied the audience into giving the standing ovation at the end.

I drove home to my apartment in East Leaside—The Canterbury Arms. It was a low-rise and if I could describe it in one word it would be 'rusted.'

Before entering, I stopped at the park bench in front of the building. Sitting there, as usual, was a white-haired man with chalky skin and a frail body. He had been an actor who'd come out to California when he was young to make it big in the business. Never happened and now he was homeless and holding up the tin cup that I had given him.

"Hey, George."

He smiled showing off a mouth full of nothing.

"Having a good day?"

"Sure am, Joshua."

I stuffed twenty bucks into his tin like always. It didn't matter how well or how poorly I was doing at the time. I always felt that I was one step (maybe half a step) away from being in his position.

I entered the building and walked a flight of stairs to my apartment. I live in a bachelor. Let me replace that with 'inhabited.' No one really 'lives,' in a bachelor. It was tiny and the walls were plastered with posters from movies I'd had bit parts in. Whenever I felt down, I looked at them to inspire me. The furniture was a second-hand couch and a TV that I had to hit on the side to turn on and off. I had a hunch Johnny Depp didn't live this way.

I was exhausted, but I forgot all about it when I played my answering machine messages. It turned out my agent, Biggie, had phoned with great news. I had made it to a second audition on the *Hamlet* gig. I get excited when I hear news like that so I replayed the message several times that night. Then, another few times in the morning. Of course, while I was shaving, I listened to it once or twice more. Okay, I guess I go a little overboard, but it's not every day I get a callback. Biggie ended the call by saying he wanted me to come into the office on Saturday.

I figured he probably had some projects that would help jump-start my lagging career. Sure, *Dirty Old Men*, was a fine theatrical piece, but there was more I wanted to do.

On Saturday, I stood in front of the gleaming metal and glass structure that housed the office of The Robert Bigalow Theatrical Agency. I took the elevator up to the sixth and began walking down the hall, when Rex Lawson, with his perfect posture, perfect long blonde hair and face full of perfect cheekbones exited.

"What's up man?" he asked.

"Oh, not too..."

"I've been pretty busy. Just finished *Little Women* on Broadway, then did a turn on the TV show *Handsome Guy* and, of course, I appeared in that film *Winter Ramblings*. I think it's going to be nominated for an Oscar. Tomorrow, I start work on that TV show, *Psycho Baby*, a comedy about Freud's early years." He smiled, showing his snow-white teeth. "Great talking to you, Josh." Then he walked away.

He kinda put me off wanting to stay in the acting profession, especially when all I seemed to get was

'Dead Man #3' or the occasional role in a mouthwash commercial where I'd get cast as bad breath.

I walked into Biggie's office and headed over to the reception desk. The waiting room was small, but it made up for it in atmosphere. There were numerous photographs of celebrities adorning the walls and it made me feel as if I was in the heart of show business. You could smell the glamour, the excitement and the sex. Maybe that last part came from Biggie's beautiful red-haired receptionist, Charlotte Weaver. She had pouty lips and a figure that could make a Victoria Secret girl weep. I lobbed her a big sexy Mclintock smile, but didn't get a return.

"He's waiting for you."

"Charlotte, I just wanted to say..."

She scowled, then pointed to the office door. "Go."

Past history.

I shrugged and entered.

As always, Biggie slouched behind his small desk cluttered with scripts, glossy photos and contracts. Yes, his desk was messy, but he, himself, always looked professional—nice suit, probably Armani, short, black hair combed back and a complexion that seemed as if he set the tanning booth dial on fry.

"Great to see you, Joshua. Have a seat."

I sat down and he picked up a file on his desk, looked through a few pages. "Okay, so your callback for the *Hamlet* audition is Thursday at eleven, Indigo Studios."

"Eleven in the morning?"

"Yes. Problem for you?"

"Uh, no, no, no." Actually, that should have been, "yes, yes, yes," when I thought about what Lowenthal would say when I asked for another morning off. Actually, he probably wouldn't say anything because he'd be too busy sticking a knife in my back. "I just wondered Biggie..."

He sighed. "You're not going to ask me again are you?"

"Did you try?"

"Yes, I tried. Like I try twenty times a year." He spread his hands. "Joshua, the Leaside Repertory Theatre is not interested in having you audition at this time."

"Did you tell them that I would be great as King Lear? It's the part I was born to play."

"Yes."

"And did you mention all the movies I've been in?"

"Yes."

"And what about..."

He leaned close. "Joshua, they don't want you."

My whole body sagged.

"Don't worry about it. I have something better for you." His hands dived into the pile of papers on his desk and pulled out a somewhat crinkled, coffee-stained script. "Take a look at this."

He tossed it to me. The title was 'Doctor Chip.'

"A medical show? That could be my breakthrough role. That's the way Clooney started on *ER*."

His big shoulders swayed a bit like they weren't sure which way to go. "This is a little different. It's about a doctor who gets arrested for malpractice and then becomes a Chippendale dancer to make ends meet."

I riffled the script. "Interesting." Of course, I would have said, 'interesting,' if it was about a monkey who wanted to be Governor. I just wanted to work.

"Oh, and here's your check from that indie film you did, *Nude Bikini Models*."

Biggie handed me a small white envelope. I stuffed it into my pocket and leaned back in my chair. "I never really understood that movie, Biggie. I mean if they're nude, how can they be bikini models? They can't be both." That was one of the philosophical issues I wrestled with while learning my lines. Of course, once filming started, none of the girls were wearing anything at all and it didn't seem to matter so much to me anymore.

I headed out of the office and down the stairs. When I got outside, I opened the envelope Biggie had given me and stared in shock. I had an emergency situation on my hands.

Chapter Three

I got into my car and drove to The Screen Actor's Guild office or SAG as it's often called. It closed at six so I had to step on it to get there.

I made it with five minutes to spare and entered the small white-bricked building. Marcia was locking the office doors so I raced inside. "I have to see Kennedy," I said.

"Joshua, we're closed. Especially to you."

I guess I deserved that. Kennedy and I had had our differences in the past, like the time I came here in a drunken stupor and tried to show him some new moves I'd learned in Salsa class. Kennedy had seemed appalled, although it might have just been because I wouldn't let him lead.

"It's important," I yelled as I tried to pull the door open while Marcia attempted to lock it.

"Kennedy is busy."

"It could have huge ramifications for the entire industry."

She blew out air as she looked at my twinkling blue eyes. At that moment, I knew she couldn't refuse.

"Alright, but make it quick."

She opened the door and I headed over to Kennedy's office.

"Wait, I have to tell him first."

I turned around. "Sorry, Marcia, if you tell him, the element of surprise is gone."

She looked puzzled, but I'd learned that to get what you want it's important to surprise people. Once they know who you are, they might not let you in. I 'seized the day,' like Robin Williams in the movie, *Dead Poet's Society*, and dashed into the office.

Kennedy was standing by the wall, pinning articles about films in production onto his already full bulletin board. He looked like a corporate drone, with his crew cut, pale face and small black glasses. Although he was in the movie business, his position was basically administrative so he didn't have the pizzazz usually exhibited by showbiz folk.

He turned to look at me, a sour expression filling every nook and cranny of his face.

"Mclintock? What are you doing here?"

"I have to talk to you about something."

"Didn't Marcia tell you we're closed?"

"This is important."

"Look, Mclintock, I've got things to do. After I finish here, I have a meeting with studio executives about increasing DVD residuals. So I really don't have time to chat."

"But..."

He glared at me. "Wouldn't you have wanted a decent return for your performance in *Seahorse*?"

I couldn't believe he was throwing that in my face. *Seahorse* was a movie I wanted to forget. I played a miniature jockey riding on a tiny seahorse in a race. It was the lowest point of my career so far. And that's saying something. "Yes, but this could be vital for other actors to know about."

He took off his glasses, and rubbed his tired-looking eyes. "Alright what is it?"

"I sat down on the fake-leather chair in front of his desk and swiveled toward him. "Some months ago, I appeared in the film *Nude Bikini Models*. It's about these bikini models who are..."

"I'm sure it's a deep exploration of the human

psyche, but you don't need to go further, just tell me what your problem is."

"The thing is, I got my check today for my work on that film and they've tacked on administration charges. As I understand from Guideline 302, Subsection 643, they're not allowed to do that."

He blew out air. "It's allowable, under certain circumstances. How much?"

"Nineteen cents."

Hard to believe as it seems, he looked at me like I was crazy.

"Nineteen cents? You're worried about nineteen cents?"

"It was my nineteen cents. I could have used that to further my career in some way. They had no right to charge it."

A lot of emotions seem to fly through his face all at once—anger, hate, rage, disgust. I guess he couldn't understand how an actor could be taken advantage of like that.

"Get out."

"What?"

"Get out of here. And don't come back."

At that moment, I could tell his old mood swings were back. I'd experienced them on several occasions. I decided to leave and talk to him again when he was more stable.

I went home and had a great sleep, dreaming about how I would be the next big thing. I didn't know that it would happen in a different way than I thought.

The next morning as usual, I went to work at LLG. I made a few calls, but no one was buying magazines at that time. I saw Lowenthal and decided that the morning was the best time to tell him about my audition on Thursday. You know—before he knew what hit him. I was about to go over when I saw him chatting with a police officer.

I thought about asking the officer for a critique of my performance as Officer O'Toole, in the Serendipity Production of *Cop on the Take*, when Lowenthal noticed I was in and tromped over. The policeman followed.

"Mclintock, this officer would like a word with you."

The officer took a plastic bag out of his pocket that held a watch—a watch that looked very similar to the one I wore every single day of my life. It had been a gift from my ex for our first anniversary. But oddly enough, as I looked at my wrist, I noticed it was now missing.

"Is this yours?" asked the cop.

"Could be."

"Are your initials, J.M?"

"Yeah."

"Then I'm afraid you're under arrest."

Chapter Four

"Arrest? Why?"

"This watch was found beside Mr. Wallace P. Greg's dead body. You have the right to remain silent, the right to..."

I didn't hear the rest of it. I was too shell-shocked trying to figure out what was going on. Then a strange thought hit me right on the noggin—I had a callback to go to. Oh, I know murder's a big thing, but so is an audition and I sure as hell wasn't gonna let a little something like being under suspicion for murder wreck my career. After all, I could always turn myself in tomorrow—couldn't I? So, as the officer escorted me to his car, I bolted out of there, like a cat chasing a mouse. I didn't dare look back and just kept on running. But I could hear the slapping footsteps close behind me. I held my nose and scurried down a dirty alley full of old newspapers and half-broken whisky bottles. Then I dashed out into the street. I don't think my heart had beat this fast since I did that love scene with Monica Stevens in the film, *Lust in Space*. (It was a family film. Really!)

I ran down a long stretch of pavement and as I did, I realized how out of shape I was. I was puffing like an eighty-year-old man with emphysema. Finally, I knew I had to stop. I dashed around the corner between Donahue and Casson Street and caught my breath in front of Le Mode Fashions. I may have looked bad but as I peered around the corner, I saw that the cop looked worse. He was stooped over and his cheeks were red and puffed out like an Australian Blow Fish.

I didn't know what to do. If I was caught, he'd throw the book at me. I decided to use my last ounce of energy and scale the building I was leaning against.

This may have seemed an odd decision to you, but I had climbed this brownstone twice before for a radio promotion. Only then, I had been dressed as the 'Human Fly.' The first twenty people who came up to me and mentioned the phrase, 'I Love Vicker's Decongestant,' got a free bottle of the stuff. So I knew this building like the back of my hand. It was a bit of a struggle now, but once I started, there was no turning back and after a few minutes, I had made it to the top.

I looked down from the red-bricked roof and saw the officer scan the streets. He did this for a few moments, then went back to his car, a look of disgust on his face. I felt sorry for him. After all, what was a forty-year-old cop doing chasing actors across the city? Then again, what was a forty-year-old actor doing being chased?

I waited until he drove off, then quickly maneuvered myself down the side of the building and grabbed a taxi that had been waiting at the curb. I didn't have the energy to walk back to my car. The cabby gave me a strange look. He must have seen me on the roof.

"Actor," I said. He nodded and smiled. I figured out a long time ago that I could get away with almost any bizarre activity by just saying that one word. It seemed that people understood that actors were nuts so it explained a lot of behavior, especially mine.

When I got back to my car, I gave him what I thought was a pretty good tip—don't pick up actors, most of them don't have any money.

I drove over to the Seaton Tower Building which was part of the Oxbury Mall, a new development. I took the elevator to the third floor and entered Indigo Studios for my callback. It was a small office, but you didn't notice that so much as posters from various movies filled the walls. I remembered several of them including *The Big Bounty*. As I looked at the picture of Rachel Evens wearing only a towel, I smiled, thinking back to the wonderful times she and I had had together.

I told the receptionist with peach-colored hair and the pin in her nose that I was here for the callback. She ushered me into a small room with just a chair.

As always, I felt a bit anxious. Most books say it's important to be nervous performing. It gives you that great energy that makes your performance pop. And I was popping all over the place.

A moment later, a tall man with sideburns so long they looked like they could eat you appeared.

"Mr. Mclintock?"

"Yes."

"Please sit."

I sat down, ready to act up a storm.

"Okay, now, give me dead."

"Hamlet dead?"

"Yes, we're working on a new, more avant garde version."

Oh, no. Not another dead man role. That was the third one this month. Dead guy on ground, dead guy on couch, dead guy on top of dead guy. But rule number one is always give the director what he wants. I leaned my head forward, opened my mouth and showed glazed eyes. I believe I gave a masterful performance and I think critics would be raving about how my dead Hamlet seemed more alive than the other characters who were living and breathing. I stayed like that for a moment. Then the man thanked me and told me I could go.

"That's it?"

"We'll be in touch."

I headed out the door and to my car, figuring I had

aced it.

When I got home, I checked the answering machine to see if there was any word from Biggie about the audition. Sometimes casting agents phone the agent immediately if there's good news. But the little red light wasn't on. I decided to take a nap. Acting takes a lot out of you. I mean you have to reach into your very soul to bring the proper emotional angst to the part.

I lay down on the couch, closed my eyes and took a couple of deep breaths. I felt myself drifting into a deep sleep, dreaming of rainbows and puppy dogs and apple pie and...suddenly, I heard the sound of wheels screeching outside my window. My eyes sprang open. Damn those kids. I got up to open the window and yell at them again about respect for the bylaws, when I saw two large police officers, both of whom made Mike Tyson look like a ninety pound weakling, marching toward the building.

Call me crazy, but I had a hunch they might be trying to find me or some other actor who they mistakenly thought killed someone. I began thinking that maybe I should have turned myself in, but after a moment's thought, I realized it was too late for that. I ran out the back door of the building. I worried about taking my car, as they might already know the license plate number. But, as luck would have it, a cab sat waiting for someone on the street. The swarthy driver gave me a look.

"Mr. Rothman?"

I nodded and got in. I would repay the favor to Mr. Rothman if he was ever on the run from the cops for a crime he didn't commit.

"You wanted to go to Forsini's?"

I forced my brain to think. I needed some place to hide out for a while. Some place safe. Then it hit me and I gave the cabbie the address of the one person I knew who would help me.

Chapter Five

The cab stopped at 142 Ramsey Blvd. I dashed to the front door and rang the bell.

The door sprang open and Randy stood in front of me. She still looked great with her long black hair and flawless complexion. I peered into her mysterious opal eyes and wasn't sure if I saw surprise, anxiety or love.

"Hey Randy," I said, giving her my sexiest smile.

"Joshua, what's wrong?"

"Nothing's wrong."

"You only come to me when something's wrong."

"I miss you; that's all."

"Oh, really? That's not what you scrawled on my Mustang after the divorce."

"I was upset."

"Uh huh."

"Listen, uh, could I stay at your place for a few days?"

"I knew there was something. What happened? One of your little girlfriends had a party and she didn't invite you?"

"No. I'm wanted for murder."

After her initial shock, Randy said yes. Actually, her exact words were "I don't know." But I'm not really a detail person and scarcely heard them.

I had her sit down on the couch and told her the whole story. She 'ooed' and 'awed' at the right places and it was almost like I was doing my own one man show. Only this one man show was my pathetic life at the moment. As I watched her reactions, I realized she was still as beautiful as the day she'd divorced me. Actually, I did her a favor by letting her go. As soon as I did, her personnel business picked up. And now, she was very successful at finding jobs for CEOs and executives of major corporations.

Even after all we'd been through, Randy and I still clicked. And at times like this, I wondered why I didn't just give it all up and say, "Honey, I'm home." But I couldn't. The reason we split up was that she couldn't stand the ups and downs of an actor's life. But as I explained my present situation to her, it was almost like old times. On the downside, she still had Tina, her damn cat that seemed to hate me.

"Really, I didn't do it, Randy."

"You may not have been the perfect husband, but I know you wouldn't hurt a fly—unless, of course, he stood in the way of a good part."

I smiled, trying to make myself look vulnerable, but I don't think it worked.

"You can stay here tonight. But I think it's best if you turn yourself in. It's only gonna get worse the longer you wait."

As usual, Randy was right. I had to turn myself in. And I made plans to do that in the morning. But that night, I saw a late movie about an innocent guy who got arrested in Mexico and never made it out of the big house. Okay, so that was Mexico. But was there any difference?

Randy made me sleep on the living room couch, even though my first choice had been the bed—with her. But I got voted down.

I began reading the 'Doctor Chip' script Biggie had given me. It made you laugh, cry and want to boogie at the same time. Having studied tap, jazz and hip hop, I felt I could knock the dance scenes out of the park. I got about half-way through the script, then began getting drowsy. I guess running from the cops had tired me out. Criminals really need to keep up their cardio.

I had a restless night dreaming that I was in a chain gang attached to fifteen other convicts who were also actors who were innocent.

In the morning, I awoke with cat on my face. Not a good way to wake up, unless of course you're another cat.

I went into the kitchen and saw Randy eating breakfast. "Morning, honey," I said, giving her a seductive smile.

She glared at me. "Randy will do."

Wow. It may have been hot outside, but in here it was like one big ice cube.

And yet I felt the sparks flying between us left, right and center. Just like the old days. I thought that maybe the coldness was just a bit of acting. Sometimes people didn't want you to know what was going on in the deepest part of themselves. I sat down at the table, stuffed a napkin into my shirt and waited for breakfast. I usually frequented restaurants and fast food places so it would be great to have a home cooked meal.

A moment later, she dropped two eggs onto her dish. Then she handed me a glass of water and a plate with some bread on it. Bread and water? What was up with that? I guess she could see my puzzled look.

"That's to remind you that I can't have a criminal living in my house. If people find out, it could screw up my business."

"I'm not a criminal. The cops just think I did something that I didn't."

"That's why you have to go down to police headquarters and clear it up."

"They won't believe me."

"You're an actor. You can get them to believe you."

I sighed. "Look, they found my watch at the scene of

the crime."

She stared at me. "Your watch?"

"Yes."

"The one I gave you for our anniversary?"

I nodded.

"If you didn't do it, how did it get there?"

"It took the bus. How the hell do I know? But the officers had it when they came to arrest me."

She glared at me, like she didn't believe a word I said. You know what? As I listened to myself, I'm not sure I would believe it either. "I didn't do it, Randy. Really."

She nodded, a suspicious look on her face. "I have to go to work."

She didn't say anything else, just picked up her coat and left.

Well, she was right. I had to clear everything up.

But first I needed to relax a little. Yesterday's chase with the cop had been very stressful. Then there was having to sleep last night in unfamiliar surroundings without a woman beside me.

I went into the living room, sat on the leather couch and turned on the TV. Of course, the first show that popped up was about a criminal who had been locked up for ten years because he ran from the cops. I couldn't allow that to happen to me; I had three more auditions this week. I turned the channel a bunch more times and found *Sponge Bob Square Pants*. I always found watching that show a learning experience. Sponge Bob used all the emotions of the modern man. If you looked closely you could go behind the actor's mask and see the various methods he used to make himself appear angry or excited or worried. As I watched this expressive sponge, I'm sure my subconscious absorbed the many subtleties of his technique.

Of course, the actor I admired most was Robert Deniro. I had based every dead guy I'd ever played on his performances. He was truly a genius of the thespian world.

I got so involved with watching TV, that time went faster than an apple fritter at a sugar-holics convention. I had told Randy I would have the police thing all cleared up today, but now I was thinking that maybe it wasn't going to happen. Oh, I know what you're saying,—he's just procrastinating again. But I really was gonna do it—soon. Real soon.

I decided I would make a nice dinner for Randy in appreciation for letting me stay here. Maybe it would rekindle some of the magic we had and who knows where that would lead.

I looked through all her cupboards and fridge to see what she had available. I decided to make 'Chicken a la Mclintock,' and my world famous cherry tarts for dessert. I began by cutting the cherries into the shape of hearts. I learned that in the course I took on the art of seductive baking. The ovens weren't the only thing that over-heated during that class.

I slid the tarts into the oven, then while I waited for them to get done, I phoned Biggie to find out about the *Hamlet* audition.

"Joshua, I'm glad you called. A policeman was in today asking questions about you."

"Oh?"

"He wanted to know where you might be."

"What did you tell him?"

"I assumed you were home."

"Good."

"What's going on, Joshua?"

"Uh, I can't, uh, tell you."

"Are you home?"

"Look, Biggie, the less you know about me, right

now, the better. I'm sure everything will be cleared up in the next day or so. Any word on that audition?"

"Uh huh. They called this morning. You didn't get the part."

"I didn't get the part of a dead guy?"

"They said they went another way."

"He's dead!!! What other way can they go?"

"They said you were too dead. They wanted a more spirited dead guy."

"That's unbelievable."

"Did you read the script I gave you?"

"Not completely. I should be finished tonight. But what I read seemed promising." Just then the oven timer screamed. "I gotta go, Biggie. I got some tarts in the oven."

He laughed. "Oh a threesome, eh?"

"No, I really do have tarts in the oven."

"Oh," he said, in a puzzled voice. "Well, I'll talk to you later."

I hung up, upset about another job I didn't get. And for playing a dead guy yet. I guess the chase with the cop ruined my timing and I wasn't able to give that special, "Mclintock" touch to the part.

I reached into my pocket and took out a box of wine gums. Since I couldn't drink alcohol, I figured they were the next best thing to sooth my depressed psyche. At least I wouldn't end up kissing the priest at The Leaside Presbyterian Church like last Christmas.

I sat down and thought about the bad news Biggie had just given me. Maybe someone who wasn't in show business would have been worried about being mixed up in a murder case, but I was more concerned with the bad performance I had given at the audition. In the old days I used to think I'd be a star, but now at forty-one, those Hollywood dreams were dissolving like Alka-Seltzer in water. After twenty years in the business, what did I have to show for my life? No wife, no kids, no home. I had devoted myself to my craft and now that things hadn't worked like they should have, I had nothing but some wine gums to comfort myself with. But I couldn't think about that now, I had chicken to make. I rubbed the bird with oil, then sprinkled on some basil, rosemary and garlic.

I had often made dinner for Randy. That was one thing she loved about me. She was always the bread winner in our family and I guess it meant a lot for her to come home to a hot meal.

An hour later, she arrived and it reminded me of old times. She looked a bit frazzled, but when she smelled the melodious blend of flavors emanating from the kitchen, a smile spread across her face. "You cooked?"

"Come." I clasped her hand and pulled her into the small dining room. I had turned the lights down low and set the table with scented blue candles. In the middle of the table sat a bottle of Merlot and a picture of us kissing from our happy years together. I considered that one through seven. She considered that one through...one.

Her eyes took in the table and I saw tears beginning to drift down her cheeks. She rubbed them away, but she couldn't hide her joy.

"This is wonderful." She moved closer to me and I waited for her lips to brush mine, sending hundreds of tingling sensations throughout my nerve endings. But there was no brushing, no tingling sensations, no fun for my nerve endings. She walked right past me and sat down at the table.

"How come, Joshua?"

"Just to thank you for letting me stay here."

She didn't say anything, but I could see she was touched. I got the chicken from the kitchen and served it on a silver tray. "Your meal, madam," I said, in the

English voice I had used as Chauncey, the crime-solving dog for that animated TV series. Even though I was the star, the other dogs had more lines. What was with that?

I uncovered the chicken and I could see Randy's nose flail as she inhaled the delicious aroma. If eyes could smile, hers did.

I sat down across from her and we began eating. I gotta admit it tasted wonderful. And sharing food with Randy gave me a special feeling inside. It reminded me of that warm moment in the movie *Alien Blood*, when Kratu the Conqueror reunites with his brother who had lost his third tentacle. My eyes started to moisten remembering the scene.

"You've still got your touch, Joshua. It's wonderful."

"Thanks. So how was work?"

"The usual. Although, I did manage to get one of my clients a great job at IBM."

I patted her on the hand. "You always were good at what you do."

She smiled like she used to when we were together. A content smile, happy to have her loving husband beside her. We both enjoyed this loveliness for a few more bites of food, but then the mood changed. She surprised me with a right hook of conversation.

"So you worked it all out with the cops?"

"Oh, uh..." I looked at her and realized I had to give it to her straight, or maybe slightly curved.

"Uh, yes, yes I did." Okay, I know I lied, but what could I do? I didn't think she'd understand that these things have to be done at the right time.

"I'm glad for you Joshua. I know in the old days you would have procrastinated about something like this, so it's great to see how you've grown as a person."

My subconscious wanted to confess—really. But I

think my conscious had him tied up in a back room somewhere. "Thanks for noticing."

"So I guess you want to get back to your life. You probably have lots of acting things to do."

"Oh, uh, yeah, sure."

"So you'll be leaving tomorrow?"

This wasn't going the way I thought it would go. I assumed after this meal she would beg me to stay. "Not tomorrow exactly. See, it's not that simple."

"But the police know you didn't kill that man."

"Yes, of course, but, uh, they need me to lay low for a few days so that they can get the real murderer to relax a bit, think the cops have forgotten about him. Then they swoop in and arrest him."

I said all this with a straight face, but inside I felt terrible. Still, I comforted myself with the fact that I wasn't lying. I was acting. And probably should have received an Academy Award for it.

"That's fine. Just make sure you're out by Friday."

"Friday?"

She put down her fork. "Yeah, mom will be in town and I don't think you and her...uh, mesh too well together."

Chapter Six

Doctor Feldman leaned back in his chair and wiped the mustard stain off his blue oxford shirt. Why did stains always end up on his protruding stomach bringing attention to the area?

He looked at his Philippe Patek watch and sighed. It was eight-thirty already. His patients would start coming in less than thirty minutes. He wasn't looking forward to the complainers and the crazies and the eccentrics. As Leaside's 'psychiatrist to the stars,' he had treated everyone from Andy Dick to Robert Mitchell, the lead in the new blockbuster *Transformations*. You'd think with all their success they'd be happy. But no, they were a bunch of crybabies.

He felt the black dog of depression starting to infiltrate his brain, but then he heard the magical words on the small TV that sat behind his desk. "And they're at the post..." Doctor Feldman smiled, the black dog departing. Then he focused his eyes on the sturdy legs of Number Six.

Chapter Seven

The police were after me, and now I had to worry about something even scarier—Randy's mom, Edith.

"She comes down from Orlando every year."

This wasn't good. I still remembered the day Randy had told her mom we were getting married. Edith gave her the look of someone who had just eaten some bad meat. She equated actors to homeless people. Of course, now that I thought of it, I was kinda homeless at the moment. That was really not going to make a good impression on her. She hated show business, and never watched TV. Part of it had to do with her husband leaving her for a Vegas show girl sixteen years ago. I knew I couldn't be here when her mom blew into town, so it was important to figure out what I was going to do about the mess I was in.

But what could I do? I'm not a detective, didn't even know how to solve the case of the missing butter tart when my relatives came over for Thanksgiving. The thief turned out to be my Uncle Lou. I should have guessed since he was the only one with butter tart on his fingers.

I went into the backyard and sat in one of the lawn chairs to figure out my next move.

Nothing came.

But in the morning, sleeping alone again, it popped into my cranium. I would research Greg, the dead guy, like I researched people for my auditions. I'd figure out what happened to him, then go to the police and explain it all. I would get off on all charges and perhaps receive some kind of medal of honor for my great investigative work. Yeah, that could happen. The only issue was that I had to do it by Friday—which would put a little extra pressure on me. But I could do it. It was like that time I played a coroner in a student film. To prepare, I got a medical examiner to let me watch him carve up a body. By the time he finished, I had learned a lot. Like it's better to faint on your back than your side. You don't mess up any of your delicate facial features that way.

I decided to start by going to the library and looking up anything I could on Greg. I worried, however, if any police saw me, they might notice my license plate. I knew what I had to do. I popped open my trunk and rummaged through the years of junk that was there. Stuff I'd kept from various movie sets I'd been on. It brought back a lot of memories. After ten minutes, between the double-F brassiere and the three penises from *Crazy Sexy Aliens*, I found what I was looking for—the license plate I had used in the movie *Chased by Bwana*. In that film, I had to get away from another car driven by the gorgeous, Jennifer Lee Harrison. I had glued a license plate on top of mine so that Jennifer wouldn't know it was me. Sure, the car was the same, but there's lots of Hondas out there. And the fact that the plate was different would make them think it was another car. At least that's what the director said. And though I debated with him about it, when he put both hands on his head, and yelled, "aneurism!" I figured it was time to let it go.

When the movie was wrapped, I "borrowed" the plates from the car one night at 3 a.m. when no one was around. At that time I just wanted it as a souvenir. If I could have taken Jennifer Lee Harrison as a souvenir, I would have done that too.

I took the plate out of my trunk and crazy-glued it on top of my plate. Then I headed to the library. Along the way, I saw a few police cars and didn't feel nervous at all. In fact, I drove in front of them flaunting the fact that here I was a wanted man and out on the mean streets of Leaside. It was really a powerful feeling.

The library was a large white building on the side of a shopping center. I walked through the front doors, past the older than Methuselah librarians and went straight to the computers. I sat down on a hard as steel chair and searched the name, Wallace Greg. I got a chef, a dancer and a guy on Facebook who was a farmer. Amazon said I could buy Wallace Greg at cheap prices.

Then I remembered that the cop had said the name, Wallace P. Greg. That gave only one hit. But it was an interesting one. He was the owner of The Greg Theatrical Agency.

I thought I knew every agent in town, probably been turned down by most of them before I met Biggie. But I'd never heard of this one. They even had a picture of Greg. With the mole on his left cheek, crooked nose, no hair and large Dumbo-like ears, I figured out why he became an agent rather than a movie star. I made a copy of his picture and wrote down the address of the agency.

The Greg Theatrical Agency was located in a small office building above a computer repair shop. I headed up wooden stairs that looked like they could rot away while I was on them and ambled over to Number 135. Underneath the numbers, I saw the name, "Greg Theatrical."

The door was open a tad and I entered. At the front desk, sat a pencil-thin receptionist with blonde hair that seemed to have the "frizzies." I stood back, worried that I might catch them. I had a bad case of "cooties" back in the eighties and I still haven't fully recovered.

There were several people sitting on couches. The

odd thing is that they didn't look like real actors. I've been around the business long enough that I could usually tell if someone was in the profession. These people didn't seem to have that special quality that most good actors exude—an enormous ego. Of course, there are exceptions like myself.

It seemed odd that the owner had just died and yet the place still continued on, business as usual. I sauntered over to the stern-faced receptionist ready to give her a whiff of my charm, but she gave me a whiff of her charm first.

"What do you want?"

"I'm here to see Wallace Greg."

She gave me a puzzled look or maybe it was a frightened one. I wasn't quite sure.

"Can I ask what this about?"

"Sure. I, uh, met Mr. Greg at a party and he said I should come over for a talk. I'm an actor."

"Oh, uh, Mr. Greg is out right now."

The dead guy was out? How could that be?

"How's he feeling?" I asked.

"Feeling?"

"Yeah, last time I saw him he, uh, didn't look so good. Pale, white skin, seemed like he might need to lie down." I was going to say "permanently," but changed my mind.

"He's fine."

"Fine?"

"Yes, fine."

This was getting weird. "But he's out?"

"Yes, out."

"What time do you think he'll be back?"

She looked nervous. "Not for a while."

"I could wait."

"Actually, he won't be back till later in the week."

"I see." Then I looked at the people in the waiting

room. "Who are they waiting for?"

"Oh, Mr. Livingstone."

"Right, Greg told me about him. Said I should tell him my idea about a, uh, sitcom I had." Her hand reached down and I was sure she pushed a button under the desk. It would either ring a buzzer that would let Livingstone know I was here, or open up a trap door which would send me flying into the bowels of the earth. I closed my eyes just in case it was number two.

In the next moment, I heard footsteps. I opened my eyes and saw a man walk toward me. Livingstone, I presumed.

"Is there a problem, Nancy?"

He wore a dark blue suit and a wine tie with so many polka dots I felt sea-sick. His eyes were small, but he made up for it with a mouth that could probably handle half a watermelon in one bite. "This man would like to see you."

"About?"

"He has an idea for a sitcom. He's been dealing with Wallace."

"Oh?"

"It won't take long," I said. "Wallace loved the idea."

"Well, I can speak to you in a few minutes. I'm just on the tail end of something."

"Great."

Livingstone walked back into his office and I sat in the waiting room. I picked up various tabloid newspapers that were on the table and read all about Jennifer Aniston's alien baby and Hugh Grant's cemetery in his backyard. One of my dreams had always been to be famous enough so that the tabloids could make up stories about me. Maybe, "Joshua Mclintock Lives in Fridge Next to Pet Sloth Tudi, Named after Girl in *The Facts of Life*."

Ten minutes later, I was called in to see Livingstone. I walked into the too-bright room and sat down. Unlike Biggie's office, this was large and Livingstone had a perfectly clean desk.

"So what's this show about?"

"Oh, the show, right. Well, it's funny, really. Greg thought it was something that could get the network bigwigs to take notice."

He leaned back in his chair. "Pitch me."

"Well, I wasn't really intending to..."

He stared at me like a lion stares at an antelope before he crushes their skull. I moved my head back.

"Uh, well, see there's this, uh, actor and his wife. And they have a great relationship."

"What's she do?"

"Oh, this is off the top of my head, but she's in personnel."

"I can see the conflict. So she's the business woman."

"Yes."

"And he's the out of work, lazy actor who can't get any roles or when he does, fails at them miserably."

"No, no, he's not like that at..."

"I get it. He constantly annoys her with his bad habits like throwing off his clothes and leaving them everywhere..."

"I don't do..."

"And maybe wakes her up at three in the morning to tell her some great idea he had."

I was about to tell him that that was outrageous and I had never done anything like that in my life, when I remembered that I actually had done it several times.

"I like where this is going. She holds everything together and he's bad news."

"I don't know if that's..."

"How does it start?"

"Well, he's, uh, working at a part-time job as a telemarketer, and..."

I stopped a moment, trying to come up with some imaginative plot, but I couldn't think of one. I guess I had to go for the truth. "There's a murder and the police think he did it. He has nowhere to go so he asks his ex if he can stay with her."

Livingstone didn't say anything for a moment, just gave me a glazed look and crinkled eyebrows. I filled the silence with things like, "And that's the way this totally original show would go, not based on anyone or anything. Totally made up."

A moment later, a big smile appeared on his face like he was a five year old whose dentist just told him he had no cavities. He touched his finger to the desk and made an electric shock sound. "That's hot. When could I see a script?"

Actually, as I thought about it, I realized he was right. It was hot. Although, I'd have to give the actor's part a little more dignity than he seemed to think it deserved. "I'll get to work on it tonight."

"Fantastic." He stood up, came around the desk and put his arm on my shoulder. Buddies for life. "Give me a ring when you finish it. I think there's something there that I can take to Fox."

I walked toward the door, then snapped around. "Oh by the way, when do you think Wallace will be in? I, uh, wanted to ask him something."

"Oh, you know he's here and then he's not. Travels a lot. I'll have him give you a call. What's your number?"

I gave it to him. He picked up a piece of paper and wrote it down. But just like I had pretended to paint a picture when I played Van Gogh in the off, off, off Broadway production of *Can You Repeat That?* it was all show. He didn't really write anything down. He didn't intend to call me. He knew Greg was dead.

Chapter Eight

Doctor Feldman opened the door and let the tall man with the pale face in.

"Thank you for seeing me Doctor. I'm John Fitzgerald, director of the Fitzgerald Clinic." He raised his hand to shake the doctor's hand. The doctor left his hand where it was.

"What's this about?"

"A man who gets to the point. I like that. As you may know, we're a cutting-edge laboratory that specializes in treating psychiatric disorders."

"I've never heard of you."

"If you check our web page..."

"What do you want?"

"We'd like you to send some of your patients to us for treatment."

The doctor's face took on a puzzled look. "Why would I do that?"

"I think we could speed up their recovery time."

Doctor Feldman stared at Fitzgerald like he had just been released from the crazy house. "I'm their psychiatrist. I take care of their treatment."

"Yes, but our clinic has special equipment that..."

Doctor Feldman walked over to the door and opened it. "I don't think there's anything more to talk about."

Fitzgerald didn't move. "The thing is doctor we'll give you quite a substantial fee and you do have all those gambling debts."

Doctor Feldman's body started to shake. "How do you know about..."

Fitzgerald smiled for the first time since he'd been in the office. "You probably don't want any of your movie-star patients finding out about those."

Chapter Nine

I headed over to see Biggie, knowing he knew everyone in the business. I wanted to ask him about Greg's Agency.

I entered the office and saw Charlotte working on her computer. She gave me a sneer and said Biggie was too busy to see me. There was no one in the waiting room so I couldn't figure out how that could be true.

A moment later, Biggie came out from his office wearing his usual Armani suit and blue jeans.

"You busy?" I asked.

"No."

I glared at Charlotte.

I followed Biggie into his office and we both sat down.

"Biggie, I have to say, I loved that script—'Doctor Chip.' In fact, I memorized all the lines. "Yes, I am a doctor, but I do a mean Harlem Shake. Please, let me..."

Biggie didn't blink. "Sorry, Josh, that's on hold for the moment. They're re-evaluating the project."

"Oh," I said, upset, but shrugging it away. I was used to things like this happening. Still it was always a disappointment.

"But, hey, good news. I've got something better."

"Great."

"How do you feel about nudity?"

"I buy *Playboy* every month."

"I meant for you."

I gave him a puzzled look. "I have to be naked?"

"Yes. So you'd have to be in good shape. Ramp up

the fitness."

"It's a feature?"

He nodded.

"I don't know, Biggie. I have a good body and all, but..."

"You'd be working with Ben Walters, the director."

I had trouble breathing for a moment. Ben Walters. Wow. Walters had been an idol of mine ever since I was a kid. His films had made me want to be an actor. "Okay, I'm in."

He pulled a script from the top of the pile and tossed it to me.

"It's called 'Big Man on the Moon.' It's about an astronaut who eats a lot on his way into outer space. And then weighs too much to get back down to earth. It's about pain, loneliness and fat."

"Interesting. Why would I need to be naked?"

"You know the times. They're not making movies like they used to. They're all dirtied up. He's going to film the part where you're thin first, then he's going to shoot the sections where you're fat."

"I'll have to gain weight too?"

"No, he's going to digitize the fat."

"So when's the audition?"

"Tuesday at ten." He stood up, giving me the idea that I should leave. I wanted to ask him about Greg, but didn't know how to put it exactly. I didn't want him to think I was jumping ship. I was sure he'd be very upset if he thought that.

I stood up. "Just before I go, Biggie, I wondered, uh, you ever heard of the Greg Theatrical Agency?"

He gave me steely eyes. "No, never."

"Oh? I was just curious. I know most of the agencies in the city, worked for a lot of them. And I never heard of this one."

"Me neither."

"You don't know a Wallace P. Greg?"

He shook his head.

I nodded and left.

I walked past Charlotte's still glaring face, wondering why for the first time, Biggie had lied to me.

Chapter Ten

I drove home and got to work on another meal for Randy. I spent three hours in the kitchen, but it had the desired effect. She loved it. Roast beef, cheesy potato skins, and cranberry pudding. When she finished gulping it down, and drinking a few glasses of wine, she looked as content as an actor who had just gotten a star on Hollywood Boulevard.

After we finished, she sat on the couch in front of the TV and I snuggled in beside her. She was slightly inebriated, but I was the one who almost fell off the couch. I guess just being that close to alcohol affects my delicate equilibrium. Luckily, she grabbed me before I injured something important.

But the grabbing was all it took to get my body in seduction mode and alert my various organ systems to get ready for action. I looked in Randy's eyes, saw her yearnings and leaned in to lay a one-hundred-percent all-beef Mclintock lip-lock on her.

She smiled, probably knowing it was coming and preparing her hormones for the coupling. She moistened her lips. I moistened mine.

But then her moistening stopped and she spoke. "You know, Joshua, I'm really gonna miss these meals when you leave on Friday."

Leave on Friday? Brain to mouth—halt Mclintock lip-lock. I repeat, halt Mclintock lip-lock. "Friday?"

I stared at her, my lips quivering, me and them having no clue what just happened.

"Yeah, I told you, that's when mom's coming, so I

figured you'd be gone by then."

"Oh?" You'd think as an actor who had appeared in plays by Mamet, Shakespeare and Sophocles, I'd be a little more articulate. "Definitely be gone."

"Great."

It wasn't great. With the cops after me, I had nowhere else to go. In the meantime, I had a favor to ask her. "Listen, I wondered if I could borrow the card for your fitness club."

"You want to work out?" Her eyes squinted funny. "You?"

"Yeah. What's so strange about that?"

"It's just you've never done that before. Whenever I tried to get you to come to the club, you always said it was a waste of time. That we were made, how we were made. And you usually said it while you were eating a six pack of Crispy Creams."

"I just got a part that demands I be in shape."

Her eyes lit up like one of those full spectrum light bulbs. "Oh, that's fantastic. What kind of part?"

"It's being directed by Ben Walters."

"You love Ben Walters. I remember you used to talk about his movies all the time, how you would die for a chance to work with him. What's the story?"

"Well, uh, it's about an astronaut who's been deeply affected by his trip to outer space."

"Sounds like it would be pretty emotional."

"I'd be baring everything, so to speak." I had to stop talking before I said too much. If she found out I'd be naked in a film, she'd be upset, thinking this would hurt her business in some way. "So can I borrow your card?"

"Actually, I've got a Jazz dance class tonight. We can go together."

So that evening, we both got into her Lexus and headed over to Bellevue Fitness. It felt wonderful taking a drive with Randy. It reminded me of the old days.

I looked back a few times to make sure no one was following us and noticed that in the backseat there were blankets and a sleeping bag.

"What's with all the camping supplies?"

"My friend Sheila and I went up to Bear Lake last week. That's our gear."

"Oh." Then it hit me. I'm quick when I have to be. "So things have really changed with you."

Her eyes were still on the road, but I could see the side of her forehead begin crinkling. "What are you talking about?"

"There's only one sleeping bag."

Her face flushed and her voice had this edge to it. I could tell something bad was coming. I'm very intuitive that way.

"It's nothing like that. Geez, you always do that—make assumptions based on no evidence."

"It's just you never went camping when we were together."

She gritted her teeth. "Because you were so damn busy with all your stupid acting things."

And there it was, the thing that broke us up. She was upset with me because I spent so much time trying to perfect my craft and I was upset with her because...uh, she was upset with me.

Neither one of us spoke after that all the way to Bellevue Fitness, which was thirty minutes of silence. A long time. I tried to make it a little less silent by rolling the window up and down so it would make those rubber against rubber noises. But, unfortunately, she had a good car.

When we finally got there, I figured she'd have gotten over our little tiff and we'd talk again. And I was right. She glared at me and said, "one hour," through pursed lips.

I nodded and we both walked into Bellevue.

Like most fitness clubs, there was a pool, a weight room, and a steak restaurant. The restaurant was the most important because after you did all the swimming and the lifting, you could put back all the pounds you lost, thereby guaranteeing you would come back to the club for all of eternity.

I headed over to the Nautilus machines and watched everyone workout. The sweat poured off them as they pulled and pushed and probably tore a few ligaments. It got me to thinking why we actually needed machines. Cavemen never had them and they were all pencil thin. Of course, they exercised the old-fashioned way— running and screaming from Woolly Mammoths.

The room was packed with people who, unlike myself, obviously needed to be here. There were mirrors everywhere and it was a little disconcerting. Every once in a while, I'd peek at one and wonder, "Who's that great looking dude?" Then I'd realize I was looking at myself.

Of course, as always in these places, several muscle-bound freaks egotistically walked around showing off perfect pecs and enormous muscled legs. I firmly believe that if God had meant for us to look that good, he wouldn't have created chocolate.

I actually felt sorry for them needing all that attention. For me, it was enough just sitting down on the rotator-cuff machine wearing my T-shirt with the words, "Actor in *Aliens from Sigma Six*, autographs available here."

This had been my first time exercising in a year and a half. I had had physio due to my car accident, so I felt I was in good shape just sitting next to a guy who was doing a hundred leg pull-ups.

I did eventually complete the circuit training on the

machines and then had a shower. After the workout, I checked my watch and saw my hour was almost up. I thought I'd better make sure I met Randy on time. In her present mood, who knows what she might do if I was late by a quarter of a second. I left the club and headed toward the parking lot.

As I expected, she was waiting in the car, a not-so-excited-to-see-me-expression on her face. Neither one of us spoke on the drive home, but at least she put on the radio to some soft rock.

When we pulled into her driveway, I felt I had to say something.

"Randy, I'm sorry for making those comments about the camping earlier. I guess sometimes I just don't think before I speak."

She blew out air. "No, I over-reacted. It's just kind of stressful at work right now. We took on this new company and we haven't been able to get any placements yet. I'm sorry." A big smile filled her face.

"I want to thank you for letting me come to Bellevue. And I appreciate all you've done for me these last few days. I still care about you, you know."

Another smile.

I was really hitting the jackpot today.

I guess there would always be something between us. Call it electricity, chemistry, a bond, but something. Maybe even love. I looked at her, she looked at me. I silently alerted my brain that we were re-engaging the Mclintock lip-lock. I puckered up, ready to plant a soft tender one on Randy's perfect mouth. But, at that moment, she turned away and looked into the rear-view mirror. The sexual energy in the car evaporated, replaced by something else—rage. "You didn't talk to the cops did you?"

"Cops? Uh, yes, of course, I spoke to them. I mean, not in so many words and everything. But I have spoken to them—in the past and..."

"I take that as a no."

"It wasn't the right time."

"Well, maybe you'd like to speak to them now."

"What?"

"There's a police car right behind us and the officer is heading this way."

Chapter Eleven

My heart began beating like a hummingbird on steroids. "I can't talk to him now, Randy. It's too late. If they find me, they'll send me up the river or down the river or maybe even throw me in the river."

She gave me a look that could scare a werewolf. I really didn't know what to do. But then I heard the footsteps of the cop approaching the car and a thought popped into my brain. I would do the same thing any respectable criminal would do—hide. I jumped into the back seat and covered myself with Randy's sleeping bag and blankets.

I couldn't see anything, but I could hear it all.

"Excuse me, are you Randy Frickerson?" said the deep voice, I assumed to be the policeman.

"Yes."

"I'm Officer Harris. We're looking for your ex-husband—a Mr. Joshua Mclintock."

"Oh?"

"He's in a lot of trouble. Would you know where he is?"

"Have you tried his home?"

"Apparently, he hasn't been there for several days."

"Sorry, I can't help you."

"You know, ma'am, when a man does something criminal, a lot of times his ex will try and protect him—even though they may not still be together."

I had heard everything so far as clear as a bell and could tell it was all over now. Randy would give me up and I would be sentenced to life in a tiny cell with a guy named Bubba who liked beautiful men.

But then I heard the most wonderful words that Randy had ever said.

"I hate the bastard. He destroyed my life. Never did what he was supposed to do, fooled around with other women, had no steady income. He was lazy and a liar. In short, a jerk. If he comes near me, I promise, Officer, I will phone you immediately. The longer he rots in jail, the better, as far as I'm concerned. He was a lousy husband and he's an even lousier ex."

"I understand, ma'am. Sounds like a bad one. Some of these creeps just don't seem to know how to treat a lady. Here's my card. If you hear from him please let me know. We'll make sure he's behind bars as soon as we track him down."

"Good riddance to the moron."

I heard the officer's footsteps as he retreated and then the sound of a car starting. I waited a moment longer, then popped my head up from behind the blankets and sleeping bags.

"Wow, you were terrific, Randy! The way you pretended to hate me. It was amazing. Although, you may have overdone it a little with the bastard, moron stuff. But good."

She turned to look at me, spoke slowly, enunciating every word. "I wasn't pretending."

"Oh?"

"You swore you'd go to the police and clear everything up."

"Yes, well, as I said, never really found the right time."

"I can't have any of this get in the paper, Joshua. I run a business for executives. If they think I'm connected to a murderer in some way, it's going to destroy it."

"Sorry."

"That's it. That's all you can say?"

"What do you want me to say? Look, I didn't do the murder, Randy. But I have no evidence to prove I'm innocent. And if they catch me, they're going to put me in jail for a long, long time."

She stabbed the air with her index finger. "Maybe you should be in jail for a long long time." She opened the door, got out, slammed it shut. I left the car, a little afraid to follow her into the house. It was warm outside but I had a hunch inside there was going to be a big freeze.

I guess I don't have to tell you that I slept alone that night too.

Chapter Twelve

Doctor Feldman sat at his desk staring at his computer screen. He loved looking at the pictures of the beautiful women on 'Dressed and Undressed.' Sometimes he touched the screen imagining that he could feel their beautiful bodies.

But this didn't take his mind off 'the incident' with Fitzgerald. How dare he try to blackmail him into sending patients to his lab?

How Fitzgerald even knew about his massive gambling debts puzzled the doctor. He could go to hell for all he cared.

Doctor Feldman usually loved staring at the tall blonde wearing the cheerleader outfit and then looking at the next picture where only her pom poms were showing. But today he couldn't enjoy it. This Fitzgerald thing had really gotten under his skin.

Suddenly a buzz on his intercom interrupted him.

"Yes?"

"Doctor Feldman, I know you told me not to disturb you, but there is, uh, someone who wants to see you."

"Tell him to make an appointment. I'm busy."

There was a pause, then the door banged open and a burly man with a large nose trotted in.

Doctor Feldman's eyes bulged. "Tony, nice to see you. Didn't I tell you I'd contact..."

Tony "Big Nose" Spumozi pushed the doctor against the wall. "Your payment is two weeks late."

"Yes, well certain things have come up and..."

"Tony looked down at the computer screen. "Oh, my

God. You actually look at stuff like that?"

"Research for a patient."

Tony shook his head as if the doctor were pond scum. "Where's my money, Feldberg?"

"It's Feldman. I'll have it tomorrow. Three o'clock, the usual place."

"This is your last chance. If you don't have it..." Tony drew his finger across his neck making the universal sign for throat slitting.

"I'll have it. I'll have it."

Tony let the doctor go, then marched out of the office.

The doctor took one more look at the cheerleader's pom poms and shut off the internet. He picked up the phone and dialed.

"Hello, Fitzgerald. It's Doctor Feldman...I've, uh, had second thoughts. I'll send you patients, but I need some upfront money."

Chapter Thirteen

After the police showed up in Randy's driveway, it was more important than ever to prove my innocence. I was sure Biggie had lied to me about not knowing Greg so I thought I would talk to Charlotte. It was Wednesday, so I knew Biggie would be golfing at the Pike Country Club.

When I arrived at the office, she was chatting on the phone, all smiles. When she saw me, however, the smile morphed into the expression someone makes when they've been indicted. She shook her head at me indicating either that Biggie wasn't there or I shouldn't be—ever. I sat down on a chair and waited till she got off the phone.

Charlotte and I had been an item until about a year ago.

I really didn't know why she hated me so much. We had had a terrific four-month relationship. But then she got this idea in her head that we should get married. I said, "I'm not sure it's the right time." But somehow she interpreted that as, "Yes, I'd love to get married, honey." The next thing I hear is that she rented a hall and sent out six hundred invitations!

Of course, when I told her I hadn't said anything about getting married, she went all ballistic. Since then, every time I come to see Biggie, I'm subjected to her wrath. And she's like a wrath factory.

Eventually, she cooled down a bit and we could at least be in the same room together without her wanting to hire ninjas to take me out.

Finally, she hung up the phone.

"What are you doing here? You know Biggie's off today."

"I came to see you."

"Really. Now you want to see me. Well, it's too late. I'm dating Roger now. He's not perfect, but at least he wants to get married."

"I need some information, Charlotte."

"And why should I help you?"

I put my hand on hers, stared into her coral-green eyes, and spoke in my softest, most vulnerable voice. "Because deep down inside, you still care about me."

She gave me a slight smile, I guess realizing that all this bitterness toward me had really been love in disguise.

"Owww," I screamed, as she slammed a metal ruler on my hand. I looked at her puzzled. "What the hell was that?"

"That's for cancelling the wedding."

I rubbed the red rash on my hand. "I thought we were over that."

"You thought wrong."

"Look, I really need your help. It's a matter of life and death."

"Life and death?"

"Yes."

She blew out air and the grimace on her face started to soften. "What kind of information?"

I reached into my pocket very slowly, pulled out my wallet and removed the picture of Greg. "Have you seen Biggie with this guy?"

She looked at the picture. "No."

"Are you sure?"

"Yes, I'm sure."

I could see the anger making a return trip so I reached to grab the ruler. Unfortunately, I didn't count on her cat-like reflexes.

"Owww," I said, rubbing my knuckles. "What was that for?"

"I just remembered you called me on your cell phone to say the wedding was off. What kind of man does that?"

"Judging by today, I'd say one who doesn't want to end up in the hospital with tubes sticking out of his nose."

She looked back at her computer and I tried to figure out the right thing to say.

"I'm sorry, Charlotte. I really am."

She glanced over at the picture in my hand. "Who's he?"

"Wallace Greg."

Her brow furrowed. "That's not Wallace Greg."

"Yeah, it is."

"I'll admit it looks like him, but there's something not right."

"What do you mean?"

She shook her head. "I can't put my finger on it, but it's not him."

This was strange. "And you know this because...?"

"Biggie sees him from time to time."

"Here at the office?"

"Uh huh."

"Do you know when he'll be coming in next?"

She nodded, but didn't move.

"Can you tell me?"

She pursed her lips, then picked up an appointment book, riffled the pages, finally stopping at one. "I don't know why I should help you. But they usually meet here on Fridays."

"Are they meeting this Friday?"

"Yeah."

"Great, thanks, Charlotte." I kissed her on the cheek.

"I'm really sorry about everything. Can't we get past this?"

She gave me a look that said, maybe, if there's life after death.

I left, figuring that's as good an answer as I was going to get. I guess I'd never be sure where I stood with her. I just knew I had to stand a few feet back, or I'd be tortured with that diabolical device some sadist had invented.

Friday was two days away and there wasn't much I could do in the meantime with solving the Greg mystery. Besides, I needed to go to my apartment and check the mail. I hadn't been there for the last week, too frightened that the cops might be waiting. I figured that by now, my apartment wouldn't be under surveillance anymore. Just to be on the safe side, I went to my car and removed my briefcase.

In community theater, they don't have make-up artists like the fabulous Dennis Rogan. He worked on me and the other actors for *Planet of the Giant Squirrels*. (It was an underground sensation, although I got a lot of headaches when the other giant squirrels pelted me with foot-long walnuts.) So I had learned how to apply make-up on myself. I had done it for my part in *Hamlet,* and in that Christmas pageant where I played one-half of a camel. Unfortunately, my co-camel had had some dairy before the performance and suffered from lactose intolerance. It didn't end well.

I searched in my case, found my false nose, ears and beard. I also located the priest costume from when I played, Father Wally Pincus, 'Exorcist to the Stars.' I went into the backseat, and changed clothes. I even aged myself a little by streaking my hair with grey.

When I finished, I took a gander in my rear-view mirror and was impressed with my work. My own mother wouldn't recognize me. Actually, she probably wouldn't want to. We hadn't talked in years, ever since she found out that I had used the money she'd sent me for medical school to take acting courses instead. It all came out just before I was about to remove her gall bladder.

I drove over to my building, not worried about being caught by police as I still had the fake license plate glued onto mine. But just to be sure my car wasn't recognized, I parked in Roger Simonson's vacant spot rather than my own. I walked inside the building and as I waited for the elevator, Mrs. Donaldson, one of my elderly neighbors, appeared. She was about sixty and today had orange hair and an orange matching blouse. Her skirt was orange as well as her shoes. Of course, that wasn't unusual for her. Every week she dyed her hair a different color and wore matching clothes

She looked at the priest in front of her with the beard, wide nose and large ears and I figured she'd walk right by, not giving me a second glance.

"Joshua, where have you been?"

I stared at her, unable to figure out how she knew it was me under all the make-up. "How did you...?"

"What play are you doing now?"

I desperately tried to come up with a play that had a minister in the lead, but I couldn't. Then I figured she probably wouldn't know anyway. "Oh, uh, *Taming of the Shrew.*"

She moved close to me and I thought I'd been caught in the lie. "Who's Lou and why do you need to tame him?"

"Shrew."

"I am not. Despite what Mr. Donaldson says."

I figured I'd better not go further with this as I didn't want to alienate any more women in my life. "Well, nice to see you."

"You too. That grey hair is very becoming. Perhaps

I'll try that color next week." She rubbed her hair, a little orange coming off on her hands, and began walking away.

"Mrs. Donaldson."

She swiveled around.

"I wondered if there were any police here while I was gone."

She harrumphed. "As a matter of fact, there were. Actually, some strange things happened this week."

"Oh?"

"Yes, there was a break in. Our neighbor, Bernard Rumpley, had to go to the hospital. Someone knocked him out."

"What?"

"No one knows why. Apparently, he isn't missing any valuables."

"What hospital is he in?"

"Lakefront."

"Thanks, Mrs. Donaldson."

"Sure. Hope you break an ass."

"Pardon?"

"Isn't that what you actors say?"

"Actually, it's break a leg."

"Okay, I hope you break that too."

"Appreciate it," I said, smiling, hoping she'd go before she wished that I'd end up in a full body cast. After a moment, she did leave and I took the elevator up to the third floor.

I walked down the hall to my apartment and opened the door. The room was a mess. My desk had been overturned, papers scattered all over the ground and my eight by tens were everywhere. Then I noticed there was a piece of paper taped to the wall with a handwritten message. "Forget about Greg if you want to stay healthy."

Chapter Fourteen

Obviously, someone didn't want me trying to find Greg. And yet I couldn't stop; my freedom depended on it. And as a creative person, I needed to be free. If the police got hold of me I'd be put away for a hundred years. Running from law enforcement is probably the second dumbest thing to do. The first is stalking a casting agent until he gives you a part. So far I'd only done that on three or four occasions. Of course, I have to say, I have been successful at it—gotten the charges dropped every time.

In jail, life would be horrific. I'd probably be forced to perform with amateurs in a non-union production of *Driving Miss Daisy*. (With me in the Miss Daisy role.)

I picked up my mail and saw mostly bills—telephone, heat, lights. There was one bright spot—a residual check for a commercial I did advertising Wilkie's String Cheese. The only cheese string that can be eaten, as well as used to tie up garbage bags. The check was for a hundred and twenty dollars. I could certainly use that to pay off some bills. I looked at it a moment longer and couldn't believe what I saw. Another nineteen cents had been taken off for administration charges. I was enraged, but decided I'd have another chat with Kennedy when I had more time and wasn't being chased by cops.

After seeing the damage to my place, I knew I couldn't live there for a while. It was too dangerous. I would have to figure out how to soften up Randy so I could stay at her house. I left my place messy and locked the door.

I drove over to Lakefront Hospital to question Rumpley about what had happened in our apartment building.

On my way, I removed my make-up and tried to make myself feel more upbeat about things by thinking about my past performances.

It helped a bit, but I needed to work. That's the only thing that lifted my mood. Getting a job in a commercial or a TV show always perked me right up like a rock-fanatic finding some igneous. But now that I hadn't acted for a while, I felt out of sorts, depressed. I would have to bug Biggie to get me something. Anything. Even if it was 'man in car,' 'man beside car,' or 'man being run over by car.'

Rumpley's room was on the main floor of the hospital. I wasn't really looking forward to having a bedside chat with him. He was about eighty and had lived in my building for years before I'd moved in. He had short white hair and a permanent scowl on his face. He complained about everything, as well as keeping tabs on who put what down the garbage shoot. And no matter what it was, he told you it was the wrong thing. The ridiculous part was that he wrapped it up again and brought it back to you like a Christmas present.

Still, I figured he would appreciate a friendly face coming to see him in the hospital.

I walked into his room and found Rumpley laying on his bed, and, surprise, surprise, he had a sour expression on his face. One of his eyes was black and there were a few bruises on his forehead. His welcome greeting was, "What the hell you doing here, Mclintock?"

"I came to see how you were doing, Ed."

"I'll be fine, as soon as they get me out of this hell hole. I got nothing to do here. No TV, no radio."

"You can have a TV if you want."

"At these prices, forget it."

I nodded. "I wondered if you knew those guys who roughed you up?"

"No, never saw them before. One was fat and spoke with an accent. The other was short and had bad teeth."

"How'd they get in?"

He scowled. "Who the hell knows? I was watching *Dancing with the Stars*. That show is so fixed. I think they give them special shoes that make them dance better."

"They just started wrecking the place?"

"We didn't have no chit chat, Mclintock."

"Yeah, they did a number on my place too. It's a wreck."

He scowled again. With Ed that was known as a double scowl day. Of course, usually that went up into the triple digits. "Your place was a wreck already. I seen it myself when I told you to keep the noise down while you were doing that...what was it again?"

"Mime."

"Yeah, the mime." Suddenly, Ed started moving his hands around like someone had just given him a shot of happy juice. "And what's with all those wigs you have there? Are you one of those lady-men?"

"I'm an actor, Ed. I play many different roles."

He gave me a smirk. "But you like dressing up as the ladies, right?"

I figured now would be a good time to change the subject. "What were these goons looking for?"

He shrugged. "The fat guy took some shirts from my closet. I said, 'Clothes? This is what you want?' Then he pulled out my favorite leisure suit. I wasn't going to let them take that; I got married in it. So I tried to stop them. That's when they started beating me up. But a moment later, the fat guy looked at the suit and said, 'Something is wrong here.' They left right after that."

"It's odd that the only two places in the building that they wrecked were yours and mine."

He looked puzzled for a moment. "Yeah, that doesn't make sense. You and I have absolutely nothing in common."

"It might just be they were looking for me and made a mistake and went to your place."

"I don't think you're all that important, Mclintock. More likely they were looking for me." He held up his head as if he was the president of a country.

I didn't think I could get any more information so I decided to go. "Hope you feel better."

"Yeah, yeah, yeah. Scram."

This was one of my better meetings with Ed. So I thought I'd get out before it ramped up to a screaming match. When I got to the front desk, I asked the nurse when he was getting out. She said she didn't know, but that he could be staying up to a week or two more. I thought a moment, then signed over my check to the hospital so they'd put a TV in his room. I guess I felt sorry for him. He had reasons to be angry. His wife had left him and his daughter and son never called or visited.

When I got to Randy's place, I had figured out a hundred and one excuses as to why I wasn't leaving today. But then I realized that maybe I should just tell her the truth. Then, again, the truth had never worked out all that well for me.

She was sitting on the couch going through some of her business papers.

"Hey," I said.

"Hi Joshua. I thought you were gone."

"Yes, well certain things came up, and I can't actually leave right now."

She came over to me, her eyes filled with...I don't know what they were filled with, but it wasn't happy faces. "No Joshua, you have to go."

"That may be a problem."

Randy's breath quickened and she clenched her fists.

"Look if it's about me messing the place up, I'll make sure it's clean when you come home and...whatever else you'd like me to do. I'll even make you more of those dinners you like so much. You like those dinners right?"

"Yes, but..."

"Anything, Randy."

"No, it's not about that. It's..."

At that moment, another woman walked in. A woman I hadn't seen for many years and that was probably a good thing. It was Edith Frickerson, Randy's mom, and she looked about as happy to see me as a tiger whose tail you just stepped on.

Chapter Fifteen

"Mom, good to see you," I said.

I zeroed in for a kiss like a homing pigeon. She zeroed away like a moose with intimacy issues.

"I am not your mom; I will never be your mom." She shook her head violently like there was a bug in it. "You shouldn't be here. You two are divorced; there are no children. You should be out of the picture."

You couldn't argue with her, so I turned to Randy. "Uh, the thing is, Randy, I need to stay here a little longer and figure out what to do. My place has been ransacked. Someone got in and was looking for something. They destroyed a lot of stuff and if I had been there, they'd probably have destroyed me."

Edith stared at Randy for a moment and I believe she had achieved the impossible—varicose veins on her face. "He was staying here? With you?"

Randy smiled, but it didn't look real. "Just for a short time." She stood up, came over to me. "That's terrible, Joshua. Who did it?"

I shrugged. "Don't know. But they left this." I showed her the paper with the warning on it.

"I didn't realize things had gotten dangerous."

"They are. I know I seem like I can handle anything, but I'm worried about going back to my place."

I could see Randy sifting all this information through her brain. "Come into the kitchen for a minute."

When we got there, she closed the door and spoke softly. "Look, Joshua, I might let you stay if you absolutely promised that you would go to the police.

But it's mom. She really doesn't want you here."

"I know your mom hates me and I don't want to put you in an uncomfortable situation. I'll find somewhere else to go."

"You understand, right?"

"Yeah, yeah, no problem. I'll go right now." I headed toward the front door. Edith saw me and smiled. "Good, you're leaving."

"Randy's right, you two need to spend time together—alone." I did mean it, but I thought in the slightly evil part of my brain that it might make Randy think about what 'alone,' with her mom might actually be like. And that might make her rush over to me, screaming, 'Don't leave.'

I opened the door and walked down the veranda steps to my car. There was no 'screaming Randy,' so I guess I was truly leaving.

I started the car, began moving toward the street, when Randy rushed outside toward the car. I turned off the ignition and she came over to my window. I rolled it down.

"Alright, you can stay. We'll figure out something."

I got out of the car and we walked back into the house. Edith had this angry face like some garbage she had thrown out had suddenly re-appeared. "What are you doing, Randy?"

"He's gonna stay. But it won't be for long. He'll be downstairs so you won't see him. And I promise I'll go with him and make sure he turns himself in."

Her moms face twisted into a puzzled expression. "What?"

Randy turned cherry-red as she probably remembered that her mom didn't actually know that the cops were after me.

"Never mind." Randy quickly walked me downstairs to the chorus of her mother saying things like, 'You're making a big mistake,' and 'he's a loser.' She should have been a motivational speaker.

The basement was unfinished and there were all kinds of wires coming through the ceiling. The bathroom had no door. It definitely wasn't the Hilton.

"I know it's not great here, Joshua. But there is a couch. The only thing I ask is that you try to minimize the time you spend around mom. You know, I want this to be restful for her."

"No problem. I really appreciate this Randy and..."

"Yeah, fine. Just keep out of mom's way."

I nodded.

She looked at her watch. "I have to get to the office. But tomorrow we're going to the police so you can turn yourself in."

She went upstairs and I sat down on the couch. I guess it was over. I was going to jail.

My mind kept going back to what had been happening of late. There were so many loose ends. Wallace Greg looks different to different people. Biggie says he didn't know Greg, yet he is going to meet him on Friday. Then my place gets burglarized and I receive a warning about staying away from Greg.

It was all so confusing.

I told Randy that I had to work tomorrow but I'd meet her later at the police station.

The next day, I entered the doors of Silcox Studios for the naked role. I was a bit worried about it but I had cut back on my eating and I had exercised that one day so I figured I was in top shape.

I hung out at the craft table even though I felt too nervous to eat any of the food. Every production company supplied meals to its actors during the time of the production. And you could always tell by the quality of the spread what the quality of the movie or

TV show was going to be. If there was filet mignon, the production would be first class. But if there were Smarties and beef jerky, then your movie might be shown about two in the morning after an advertisement for the amazing butt-sucker exercise device.

This one had the Smarties, but at least there were many pretty colors.

Several other actors were there and amongst them was an old friend of mine—Marty Thomas. He was an actor I did the rounds with when we trying to get agents. He was short with blonde hair and a ruddy complexion.

"Hey, Joshua, good to see you, man." He gave me a hug. We actors are an emotional bunch. We have this special camaraderie, love for one another, if you will. That is unless one of us beats the other to a good part. Then we think about getting them alone and undoing all their plastic surgery stitches.

"Been getting any roles lately, Marty?" I asked.

"Just a few here and there. Actually, I've talked to some other guys and they say it's the same with them. The only one who seems to be getting stuff is Rex Lawson."

I kept my feelings to myself about that egomaniac even though my stomach was doing somersaults like it was in Cirque du Soleil.

Marty continued. "He's got something these producers like. He's always working."

I quickly changed the subject. "So what's your role for today?"

"Well, Biggie said they needed someone with my specific skills."

I smiled, getting it. "So I take it you're playing a dead guy."

"Yeah. How about you, Josh?"

"Oh uh..." I was too embarrassed to tell him that I

had to take off my clothes. "Don't know yet."

"Is it a small role?" he asked.

"I'm hoping they're not looking for small."

"It's a shame we have to take things like this. But the important thing is to maintain our dignity."

I smiled weakly. "Yeah, dignity's important." At that moment, the director came over to us. "Okay Joshua, it's time to get naked."

Marty looked at me. "Naked?" Then he started to giggle and couldn't stop.

Chapter Sixteen

Fitzgerald loved running in the park during the afternoon. Not that he was losing any weight, but it felt great to be outside in the fresh air and around the many fine dogs except the one with the big teeth who was about to chew off his leg. Luckily, moments later, the owner tugged the vicious Chihuahua away. Of course, just as that happened, Fitzgerald stepped into dog poop. Grumbling, he sat down on a park bench, took out a tissue and cleaned off his shoe.

The plan had worked like magic. The doctor had phoned him back and wanted to be part of the operation. That was funny. Doctor. Operation. He would remember to tell that to some of the other guys in "The Group." He had expected the doctor to ask for upfront money to take care of his gambling debts so it wasn't a surprise. But he had played a bit of hardball with him just the same.

He liked the name that he had chosen for his character: *John Fitzgerald* sounded solid like steel. No one would guess who he really was. That was the beauty of the whole thing. Anonymity.

He threw the tissue into a waste basket and looked at his watch. He pulled out his cell phone. "Hey, Carlos. Did Feldman send over that actress?"

"Yes, she came about three."

"Everything went okay?"

"Perfect."

"Fantastic. Feldman is going to be very useful to us. But we gotta watch him. Make sure he doesn't get...corrupted." Fitzgerald started to giggle. Carlos joined in, not understanding the joke.

"So, you want me to send in some guys to fix the doc's place?"

"That would be good Carlos. That would very good."

Fitzgerald hung up the phone and started running again, immediately stepping into more dog poop.

Chapter Seventeen

I had my robe on as a plump lady with too much makeup escorted me onto the sound stage. Angela Tompkins, a rising star in the movie business, sat on a chair, her long perfect legs crossed. I'd never worked with her but always wanted to. She was in her late twenties and a brunette. She had gleaming white teeth and oodles of cleavage that looked like it might jump out at any moment. I moved closer just in case.

She stared at me, her eyes wide. "You're Joshua Mclintock."

"Have we met?"

"No, but I saw you perform in that play up in Boston. What was it?"

"*Death of an Accountant.*"

"Great acting, but it seemed like a copy of *Death of a Salesman.*"

"How so?"

"Instead of Willy Loman, the main character's name was Lilly Boman and instead of Biff, the son's name was Kiff."

"Never noticed."

"Anyway, I don't usually give out compliments but I thought your performance was amazing."

"Thanks. Actually, I was mostly the understudy, but the lead actor got a mild case of food poisoning that night."

"You were lucky."

"Yes, luck did play a part. I was also in charge of bringing him his meals."

She laughed.

I heard footsteps and looked in their direction. A man wearing a grimace entered. Although his face was pale, his shirt looked like it was fiesta time. Reds and blues and purples and yellows and some colors I don't think had been invented yet.

"Hello, everyone. I have an announcement. Ben Walters has decided that this project is not up to his supposed high standards, so I will be directing. I am Titus Levinsky. You may know me as the director of *Hard Cheese*." He smiled and bowed. "Thank you."

I was disappointed, but I had seen *Hard Cheese* and thought it was wonderful, so I had hopes that he could bring the same magic to this one.

Titus moved his legs around as if he were going to do a pirouette, then spoke again. "I'd like to start by building your character, Joshua. I see him as a 'goat-like man.'"

I stared at him. "Goat-like?"

"Yes, unpredictable, wild, sometimes tenacious. Other times, tender and loving."

I nodded, understanding his process a little better.

"I'd like you to begin by acting as if you are a goat, Joshua."

He didn't have to ask twice. I got on the ground and start moving around, making sounds and kicking a few times.

"Kick higher, Joshua."

I kicked a few more times, almost injuring Angela.

"Okay, I want you to stand, but remember the goat."

"Got it."

"Excellent." He put his script down on the table.

"Okay, this scene takes place the night before the astronaut is going to the moon and he and his wife have an argument."

Angela and I quickly looked the scene over.

"Joshua, you're in the bathroom having a shower and, Angela, you begin by coming in the front door.

I smiled at Titus, needing to know some vital information. "Was it a cold shower or a warm shower?"

He glared at me. "What difference does it make?"

"Well, I have to know how to play it. If it was warm, I'd be relaxed and my entrance would be more subdued. If it's cold I might be shivering slightly and I'd have goose bumps all over my body."

"You can give yourself goose bumps?"

I held my head up, proudly. "I'm a trained thespian."

The director grabbed his head as if his brain just hemorrhaged. "Do whatever you want. Just make sure you stand on your mark."

I walked into the bathroom, having decided that I would play it as if I'd had a cold shower. I needed the challenge of producing goose bumps.

After a moment, I stuck my head out and yelled to the director. "Should I make pleasurable sounds as water hits me? Or maybe sing a song?"

He glared at me again, then shouted, "No!"

"But that would give a layer of authenticity to my performance and..."

It looked like another hemorrhage starting. "Fine, do whatever the hell you want."

I smiled and went back to the bathroom.

I usually wasn't nervous about performing, but today was different. The nudity thing was getting to me. But I didn't have time to think about that now. The director yelled, "Action!" and Angela stumbled in, acting as if she were drunk. She was good. I decided against doing the pleasurable sounds or singing. It didn't feel right.

I took a deep breath and exited the bathroom wearing my robe. I grimaced at Angela, "Why are you so late?"

She pouted. "Can't a girl go out once in a while?"

"It's every night."

"I have to have some kind of life. You seem to have forgotten all about me."

I looked at her, wondering how anyone could have ever forgotten Angela. "I haven't forgotten. I've been busy. When you're an astronaut you're busy all the time."

She got in my face. "Are you too busy now?"

"I'm tired. It's been a long day."

She grimaced, grabbed my robe and whipped it off, and started tearing it into little pieces. "I'm so sick of your excuses."

And there it was. I was naked.

And you know, the actual being naked part wasn't so bad. The bad part started a moment later when I heard the sounds of a fire truck and an axe crashing through the front door. Two fireman appeared holding a hose that shot a burst of water which slammed me against the wall. Yeah, maybe that was the start of the bad part.

When the water stopped, I heard the one fireman say, "Everyone stay calm! Everything's going to be okay."

Titus stared at him. "What is the meaning of this?"

"Your fire alarm went off down at the station. There's no time to waste; we got to get you outside."

I didn't see any fire, but I went back to get my clothes. The fireman screamed, "No!" then picked me up and carried me out the broken door.

A few moments later, we were all outside. Titus and Angela drove away together. I was left standing naked in front of Indigo Studios, a small crowd forming around me.

Chapter Eighteen

It turned out that the fireman had gone to the wrong address. It was the next door restaurant that had the smoke.

I finally got to go back inside and get my clothes. I got the hell out of there before the cops came and added indecent exposure to my list of offenses.

I had an appointment to meet Randy to turn myself in at eight in the evening. I looked at my watch and it was only six. So I had time to go to Biggie's office and catch a glimpse of Wallace Greg.

I decided not to go up to the office, mostly because I didn't want to get more ruler rash from Charlotte.

I parked in the underground next to a Jaguar. It seemed darker than usual down there. Some of the lights were burned out and it had a spooky atmosphere, like that movie I was in about the three horny spirits—*Ghost Lusters*.

I waited a few moments, hoping I'd see Greg. A few men entered the underground, but looked nothing like him. One was squat, but muscled with a round face. He looked like a sumo wrestler with a few extra pounds. Another was an ultra-thin woman who seemed as if she could squeeze through a sewer grate with no problem at all.

I waited about ten more minutes and didn't see anyone resembling the man Charlotte had told me about. I was about to go upstairs and ask her what happened when I felt something grab my arm. I looked over and saw the squat guy again.

"You got a light, buddy?" he growled.

"No, sorry, don't smoke. Stains the teeth, bad for close-ups." I gave him a big smile and showed off Dr. Eickman's fabulous work. He had given me a certificate that said I was his best dental patient because I didn't scream once. Not once. Of course, I did throw a few tantrums when I didn't like the color of the balloons he gave me for sitting so quietly.

"It's been a pleasure, but I gotta go." I tried to move my arm, but his grip was strong. He pulled his other arm back and gave me a fist sandwich. Let me tell you, that's not my favorite type of cuisine. I fell onto the ground, everything turning black.

When I woke up, I was on the concrete floor of the parking garage. My head hurt like I had received a thousand rejections. I stumbled up and looked into the side mirror and was almost suicidal when I saw a mark on my cheek. My face was my fortune. I couldn't have that. I rubbed it for a few moments, but it wouldn't go away.

I was so depressed, but felt better when I rubbed the mirror and found out the mark wasn't on my cheek.

I headed back to Randy's place. No one was around, so I went downstairs and had a rest. Being knocked unconscious really tires you out. I didn't get up till the next morning.

I went upstairs and Randy called me into her bedroom. I assumed she hungered for the Mclintock-lip-lock. But when I got there, she gave me the third degree. Not conducive to the M-L-L.

"Where were you last night?"

"What?"

"You were supposed to meet me at the police station so you could turn yourself in."

"Oh, right. I'd planned to, but someone knocked me out and I couldn't..."

"Someone knocked you out, huh?"

"Yes. I'm telling you the truth, Randy." I gave her a big smile. Dr. Eickman was really getting a lot of free advertising today. "I'm trying to figure out about this guy Greg and..."

"Joshua, if you don't turn yourself in, I'm going to have to ask you to leave."

I stared at her stern face and saw she meant it.

I didn't want to think about that now and went into the kitchen to get something to eat. Edith was sitting at the table, a plate of fried eggs in front of her.

I grabbed some cheese from the fridge and started chewing. Edith looked up at me like she wanted to tear off my skin and use it to make a hat. "You know you're a terrible actor."

I tried to remain calm. "Some of my work is better than others."

"I'm sure all of it's terrible."

My heart started beating fast. "Have you even seen me in a movie?"

"No, but I know you're no good."

My eyes started to moisten. At that moment, Randy walked in and I ran downstairs to my room. I slammed the door and lay on my bed feeling like a sixteen-year-old girl who had just been dumped by her boyfriend. I felt a tear start to trickle down and rubbed it away.

A few moments later, I heard a knock at the door.

"Joshua, can I come in?"

It was Randy. "I guess."

She opened the door, walked in and sat on the bed. "I know mom and you don't see eye to eye."

"That's an understatement."

"But, look, she has her opinions and nothing is going to change those."

"Unfounded opinions. She told me I was a terrible actor and she never even saw me once. I invited her all the time when we were married, but she never showed up."

"I know. I remember seeing you in that romantic comedy that took place at the Burger Palace."

"*Love on the Bun*?"

"Yeah. You were really good."

"I was?" I said this as humbly as a magnificent actor can say such things.

"Look, mom's going home in a week. I just need you to get along with her until then. Do you think you can do that?"

"I'll try."

"Try hard."

"Sure."

"We'll talk about turning yourself in later. Right now, I have to take mom to the dentist."

"He's going to sharpen her fangs."

"What?"

"Have a good time."

She left and I lay in bed thinking about my life. Not a good idea for me. It always made me feel down. To pick myself up, I took out some DVD's of my earlier work, things I had taped over the years. First, there was the Taco Bell commercial where I played third Dancing Burrito to the right. Then there was the commercial for Viagra. I played the 'before' picture where I was about to jump out the window because I hadn't had sex in a week. Thank God, that's never happened to me, personally.

Marty called and asked if I wanted to get together. He said he had some things he wanted to talk about.

We met at The Third Eye restaurant, a bohemian place out in the village. The place was new-age-y, decorated with pictures of virgins being sacrificed to Hindu gods. Nothing like that to get your appetite going. Marty was a sprouts and tofu kind of guy while

I was more of a steak, potatoes and Cheese Whiz man.
I had him order since I really didn't have a clue about
this type of food.

When our meals came, he dug in like his bean curd
loaf was a Grade A filet Mignon and his fried lentils
were Spumoni ice cream. I stared at my plate for a few
moments, the funky aroma wafting toward my nose.

"How did your, uh, nude thing go?" he asked, eating
a big chunk of bean or curd or that green thing on his
plate that slithered from side to side like it was alive.

"Good."

"I heard you got to do scenes with Angela
Tompkins."

I scooped a spoonful of the stuff on my plate into my
mouth and forced it to chew, even though I don't think
it wanted to.

"What kind of film was it?"

"Well, there was lots of action." I quickly switched
subjects. "So how did your thing go?"

"Not great. I was supposed to be Dead Body
Number Four. When I collapsed on top of the other
dead bodies, I fell on the wrong part of someone's
anatomy and the guy screamed. Ruined the take. The
director was not happy. Then when we did it again, I
fell asleep. Only I have restless leg syndrome."

"This doesn't sound good."

"It wasn't. I was supposed to have been killed by a
vampire and yet my legs were moving like I was
performing Zumba." He swallowed some alfalfa juice
like it tasted good. "I think I may have ruined myself
for getting any more dead body parts."

"Well, if you have to make a sacrifice and play live
ones, that's what you have to do."

He laughed.

"Actually, that's what I wanted to talk to you about.
Have you noticed anything different about Biggie

lately?"

"Different?" I moved my fork on my plate, not sure where it should go next—the thing that looked like a rotten tomato or the other thing that looked like a bird's nest. I took bird's nest.

"He hasn't been looking after my career like he did before. I mean he used to give me more roles. They weren't great, but I did get them. All dead guys, of course."

"Sure."

"But lately, I seldom get any calls. It's almost like he's phasing me out."

I thought about that a moment. He was right. Biggie had been a bit strange lately. I was sure I'd caught him in a lie. "Maybe there's not as many roles right now, you know, with the economy and everything."

He shrugged. "Maybe. The thing is I wanted to find out if something was going on with him. So I had my sister call and pretend she was from a production company saying they had a part for me. It was a fake call; there was no part. Biggie didn't even tell me about it."

"Maybe he just forgot."

"Have you ever known him to forget anything?"

I thought a moment, shook my head.

"I just hope he doesn't have plans to get rid of me. Acting is my life."

I took a sip of the onion tea. "I had something to ask you too. Do you know a Wallace Greg?"

"Sure, I was with his agency before Biggie."

"Was he any good?"

"They never got me a single role. Of course, Livingstone was actually my agent."

"Did you ever see Greg?"

"Once or twice last year."

I reached into my wallet and pulled out the photo I

had shown Charlotte.

He looked at it from all angles and then said, "It kinda looks like him, but his face is a bit fatter and his eyebrows lower. It's almost like aliens were trying to clone him but couldn't get it just right."

Chapter Nineteen

Doctor Feldman walked back into his office after paying off Tony. He sat at his desk feeling thrilled that that was over, at least for the time being. He had made the right decision in signing up with Fitzgerald. At least this way he'd be getting money every month and Tony would no longer threaten to break his scrotum.

His first session of the day was supposed to start in twenty minutes, so while waiting, he turned on the TV to see what the horses looked like at Belmont.

As he watched, he got an odd sensation. It was almost like he was the one being watched. But not from the TV—from his office. He looked around the room and saw nothing unusual.

Maybe he was just a bit paranoid after that run-in with Tony. Yeah, that was probably it. Although, every few moments, Doctor Feldman took a look in another corner of the room just to be sure.

Then he checked his scrotum.

Chapter Twenty

I drove Marty home, puzzled by what I'd learned. Both Charlotte and Marty had both said the same thing. The picture was Wallace Greg, but it wasn't. It didn't make any sense. Did he have some kind of work done on his face?

I decided to go for a drive to clear my head. Sometimes I do that. I just let my car take me wherever it wants. Of course, one time it took me to a Fiat dealership so that it could see the cars without their bras on. You can believe I had a talk with my car after that. Today, for some reason I ended up on the street near Greg's Agency. I left the car and was tempted to go up to his office, but decided against it when I saw a cop exit. Instead, I took a walk in the opposite direction. Ten minutes later, I felt refreshed and a little more upbeat. When I got back to the car, the fat man who had pounded me out in the parking garage was leaning against it.

"Hey, Mclintock? Great to see you again." He reached into his pocket and I had a hunch he wasn't going for some pistachios. So I started to run.

There was an alley nearby and I sped down it. But I could hear his footsteps right behind me. I managed to keep inches away, even though the energy I had gotten from the exercise I had done that one night a week ago at the gym seemed to have worn off. I didn't understand. Isn't exercise supposed to give you energy?

I scurried over the fence of a sewage plant, and jumped down to the ground. I kept running, but when I looked back, he was still there.

I turned a corner and went into an open door of the plant. I watched through the window as the fat man ran past. I waited a moment as I tried to calm my breathing. Then I headed back to the car.

I was exhausted and wanted to know what was going on. But there was nothing I could do except go home.

When I entered the house, Randy and Edith were in the living room talking. They looked at me and their conversation stopped.

"Hey, guys, you wouldn't believe what just happened. I was chased into a sewage plant by this big guy. I have no idea why or what he was after, but he was a very good runner."

They continued staring. I guess they were stunned by my news. At that moment, I realized they didn't look happy. They both reminded me of a dog when you take away its ball. It almost looked like they wanted to bite me and bury me in the backyard. Not the first time women have wanted to do that. "What's up?"

Randy spoke in her quiet voice. "We need to talk, Joshua."

"Oh?"

She said, "we," but so far Edith had not said anything. That was unusual. She just kinda looked at me with the motherly eyes of a man-eating piranha. I didn't really think that was a good sign.

I walked over to the hassock and sat down. I could feel my heart still beating from the chase with the big guy. Or was it horrified from that glaring look from Edith.

Randy leaned toward me. "Have you seen the newspaper?"

"No. Anything interesting?"

Randy nodded, but there was something ominous about the nod. Something that you expected to see in the middle of a horror movie just before the crazy psycho intended to rip someone's head off. "Yes, there was something interesting."

"Oh?"

She reached over to the coffee table, picked up *The Chronicle* and handed it to me.

I started reading and shook my head. "That's terrible. How can the banks raise interest rates? People are going to revolt. I might even join them."

I said that last part, shaking my fist, and scowling. I figured if that was what was making them so fired up, I'd join them in their outrage. That usually brought people closer together. But I looked back at them and didn't see their glacier-like faces soften any. Where was Global Warming when you needed it?

Randy snatched the paper from my hand. "Not that. This." She pointed a finger at an article a little further down the page. "Telemarketer Sought for Murder of Talent Agent." Below that was a picture of me.

I couldn't believe it. Why the hell would they choose that picture? I had so many better ones. It looked like I was drunk or stoned. I would have to write a letter to the editor about that.

I began reading and saw the article was about how I had shot a Mr. Greg of the Wallace Greg Talent Agency. They went into the fact that the evidence so far was that my watch had been found at the scene of the crime. Was that the kind of thing they call evidence? Could they really prove that watch belonged to me even though mine was gone and the inscription on the one they found, read, "To J.M., love Randy."

I think the real problem is the crappy watch straps they make today. Not secure enough. Maybe they should jail the watch strap makers. Yeah, that's what they should do.

Suddenly everything hit me. I was in the paper for

murder. Before this, it was all just a nebulous concept. Sure, I ran away from the cops, but it didn't seem like such a big deal at the time. But now seeing it in print made it 'real.' The cops were going to toss me into a cell with a big man named Bubba, who liked beautiful men.

Edith moistened her lips, never a good thing. Words were going to come. And not ones I wanted to hear. "I told you all along he was a loser. And he's still a loser."

You know, I sort of preferred her when she wasn't speaking. I leaned forward toward Randy, planted a sincere expression on my face. "I'm sorry. I'll do whatever..."

Her mom spoke again. "Loser."

Randy turned toward Edith. "Mom, can you let us talk?"

"Fine." She got up, whispered, "jerk," and then exited the room. I gotta admit it was a pretty good exit line.

Randy brushed back her hair and spoke in a softer voice. "I told you, Joshua, the publicity is bad for my business."

I thought about that for a moment. "Not necessarily. The great acting teacher, Antonio Beretski said all publicity is good publicity. Cause it gets your name out there in the public eye. People will remember you."

"Yes, well, Beretski didn't run a company that deals with scandal-worried executives. You know the climate today. The slightest thing that people do is under the microscope."

I had to admit, she was right. Beretski actually worked part-time as a meat cutter and when he accidently chopped off a customer's finger while explaining why the prices of his rump roasts were so high, the publicity overshadowed his performing career and he was never hired again—for acting or for slicing rump roasts. Actually, he ended up in an old age home where they kept him away from all the sharp objects.

"Joshua, over the past three years I have built up my reputation as a reliable, lily-white agency that can supply employees for the highest-level corporations."

I nodded. "And I have to congratulate you on a job well done."

"Yeah, well, that is not going to last long. Once they get a whiff of this, they'll no longer use my agency. My years spent building it up will have been for nothing."

"Don't worry," I said, tossing the paper onto the table. Executives don't read rags like this."

"You mean *The Chronicle*? The newspaper with the third largest circulation in America?"

I could have been wrong about that. I picked up her limp hand. "I'll fix this, Randy. I promise."

"And how would you do that?"

"Oh, I, uh, have some great ideas. I'm an actor, very creative."

"Would you like to share some of those very creative ideas?"

"Not at this time."

She pulled her hand out of mine, faster than a krill swims away from a shark. She stood up. "Joshua, I was content to let you stay here if you weren't causing any problems, but now mom and I have decided that maybe it's best you go."

"Mom too? Really? I thought the two of us were really connecting."

I could see a small smirk starting to crack through her frozen face, like ice when you pour something hot on it. That's the one thing that held us together all those years; I could make her laugh. Unfortunately, in this case, the smirk disappeared as soon as it had appeared, like a mirage in the desert.

"You're throwing me out?"

"No, not throwing. Just telling you that it would be better if you left."

It sounded like 'throwing' to me. But I wasn't going to argue semantics with her. "Randy, the cops are after me. I really don't have any place to go. If they catch me, I'll go straight to prison."

"I'm sorry, Joshua. Even if I let you sweet talk me into letting you stay, mom wouldn't go along with it."

I had always depended on Randy to help me when things got tough. I guess I'd burned another bridge. Like the time during my drinking days, when I punched that director when he fired me on set. The worst part was he toppled onto a car that was rigged with plastic explosives for an action sequence, then spent seven months in the hospital with burn marks all over his body. When he got out, I tried to get an audition with him. Oddly enough, he refused. Perhaps I just wasn't right for the part.

I looked at Randy, truly sorry for the problems I'd caused her. "I understand. I'll be out today."

I went down to my room and packed.

Chapter Twenty-One

Fitzgerald loved eating spaghetti and meat balls for breakfast. It made him feel continental. That's why he came to Figaro's Restaurante every day.

As he swallowed the last of his food, he picked up the latest issue of *The Chronicle* from his table. He stared at it a few moments, then his hands started to shake and he began breathing heavy. For a moment, he worried he might cough up that last meatball.

He couldn't believe it. Mclintock was ruining everything. He knew too much. He had seen too much. And he was bringing attention to things that shouldn't have attention brought to them. He would have to have a talk with 'The Group' immediately.

Chapter Twenty-Two

I called a couple of old girlfriends to see if I could stay with them, but they all said "no." More burned bridges. And worse yet, my financial situation was not liquid. The only place I had enough money to stay, at least for a few days, was a hotel in the bad section of Leaside called The Cameron.

The place was a dive; however, the man at the front desk didn't seem to realize it and wore an expensive suit and tie, like he was working at the Lido Hotel in Paris. What ruined the image, however, was the big smile showing a lovely assortment of broken teeth.

"Ten bucks an hour. Where's the lady?"

"No, no, just me."

He gave me an odd expression, like no one had ever come alone to his establishment before.

"And I may stay a few nights."

"Oh, extended stay." The dentist's nightmare smile returned. "Great. In that case, I can you give you the discount. But I need twenty bucks upfront."

I paid him, then went up to my room.

It was small, but the sheets looked clean. The wallpaper was composed of an endless variety of wavy lines that almost put you into a trance. Maybe this was to hypnotize you so you'd think you were at the Lido.

I needed a place I could think and I usually did my best brain work at a club. I changed into my club clothes—crushed velvet jacket, jeans, and Dockers. I went downstairs and asked Smiley at the front desk if he knew of any places in the area.

He said there was a bar down the street called "The Lock Up." I nodded and left.

I know it's a bar and I'm an alcoholic. But I knew if I loaded up on wine gums before I went, I'd be fine.

I walked down the sidewalk, passing burger joints, Shawarma places and numerous pizza parlors. As I came to an intersection, I saw an officer in a police car parked on the side of the road. I turned away, moved my shoulders up and marched forward. That's right; I was acting British. You know, like when I appeared in *Butler Jim* as servant to a pit bull who'd been left a lot of money by his master. The role went to the dog's head. In between scenes, he wouldn't let me sit on any of the furniture.

I heard a siren, then saw cop cars racing down the street to some emergency. I realized I'd better find "The Lock Up" soon or I was going to be locked up myself. I paused every few moments looking in store windows, hoping it would make me look like a normal every day window shopper.

Finally, I came to a small grey-brick building. "The Lock Up" was written in big orange neon letters on a sign in front. I was about to walk in when I noticed what looked to be bullet holes in the door. That worried me a little, but with all the cops around, I had to go somewhere.

The place was as dark as a cave. The good news was that nobody would notice me here. The bad news was that I couldn't notice myself either and if I accidently stepped the wrong way, I might trip and end up with a broken coccyx. I liked my coccyx the way it was. The further I walked in, the more the darkness receded and I could actually see many tables where grubby-looking men sat, their faces hidden by big hats. It looked like everyone was here for the same reason as me—so they wouldn't get noticed. Maybe this is where all the criminals who the police never found were hiding out. It was like the Bermuda Triangle for crooks.

I sat down at a table in the back.

"You're under arrest," I heard a voice say as I felt handcuffs encircle my wrists. My shoulders raised and this time not to be British. I was scared and I don't mind admitting that. How they found me here, and so quickly, I wasn't sure. All I knew was that it was over. In a way, I felt relieved.

I turned to look at the arresting officer and saw an attractive woman with long blonde hair. Her hair surrounded a pretty face hidden by heavy make-up. Her police jacket had her badge number as 3442. In the old days, I wouldn't have cared if 3442 was a policewoman, I still would have tried to put the moves on her. But today, with my situation the way it was, I wasn't sure it would be good form. Also, I was afraid 3442 might knee me in the groin.

"What would you like?" she asked in this sexy voice that sent shivers everywhere, especially into my coccyx.

I didn't quite understand the question. Did she mean imprisonment or torture? Did they give a choice these days?

Then my eyes followed her body downward, and I noticed she had no police pants, just legs. Long, sexy, perfectly-shaped legs ending in beautiful sexy feet in high heels. I'm not really a supporter of our police force, especially these days, but I did like the new outfits. I bet criminals jumped into the paddy wagon like fish into a net filled with bait.

The officer shook her bouncy blonde hair. "Don't look so scared, man. I'm just your waitress, Jazmin."

"Oh?" I looked down at the handcuffs around my wrists and saw that they were connected by a long metal rod to the underside of the table.

"Fits with the theme of the place—it is called "The Lock Up," you know."

I smiled, getting it. "Yes, very good."

"A lot of customers try to leave without paying. So this kinda puts a stop to that too."

I nodded. "Double purpose."

"Uh huh. What can I get ya?"

"How about a ginger ale, Jazmin?"

She gave me an odd look and left.

At that moment, my situation hit me in the face, like a pie that Moe, Larry or Curly had thrown. I was handcuffed to a table in a place where criminals hung out. Not the best position for me to be in.

Jazmin returned a few moments later and unlocked one of my hands. I asked her about the other. She told me they only do that when I leave.

As I began sipping my ginger ale, I noticed that while it was still dark back where I sat, lights had been turned on in the front area. Everyone sitting at the tables was still pretty well in darkness, but I could now see a stage. A moment later, a girl in a bikini appeared and started dancing. It was my waitress, Jazmin. I didn't really notice much about her dancing skills, although I'm sure they were grand, but my eyes were more focused on her taking off the bikini. I was astounded by her perfect body and felt like weeping and thanking God for his wonderful work. He was indeed the greatest architect, much better than the guy who designed the new Art Gallery.

This crowd did not make a sound—no whistles, cheers, applause. Perhaps they'd never seen a naked woman before.

Several more women performed, but I liked Jazmin best and was hoping she'd come back to my table.

A few moments later, I noticed men wearing police outfits wandering "The Lock Up." I thought at first that they were the male equivalent of the waitresses, but then I saw that they had pants and weren't wearing high heels.

They were real policemen!

I had to get out of there. I jumped up from my table and attempted to head toward the door, only I had forgotten that one hand was still handcuffed. As I moved, I began pulling my table with me. It made squeaky sounds on the ground. I really didn't think I'd make it out of there attached to the table. And I feared that both of us would be arrested. So I froze like a chameleon, hoping not to be noticed. However, no matter how much I willed myself, I couldn't make my face match the dark brown wallpaper.

Suddenly, one of the police officers looked in my direction, then he rushed toward me. I slid underneath the table. I thought I was safe, but a moment later, I saw policeman shoes move toward me.

I waited to be arrested for real this time.

Chapter Twenty-Three

Well, I had given it a good shot. I just hoped the fact that the police found me in a strip club wouldn't get splashed across the papers. That could ruin my chances of getting an audition with the Leaside Reparatory Players, as well as playing half a sheep in this year's Christmas Pageant at Overdale Church.

But as I crouched underneath the table, my full weight on my knees in what I believe was the Lotus or, as I like to call it, the "AAAAAAhhhhh" position, I saw another pair of shoes. Only these were the high heels that I'd seen before.

I stayed still and listened.

"Are you sure about that, Jaz?" said the cop, I assumed.

"I know all the regulars. If there were someone fitting that description, I'd definitely notice them."

"Yeah, I guess. Well, if you see him, call me, okay?"

"Gotcha."

A moment later, policeman shoes walked away and high heels' face appeared under the table. Jazmin licked her lips and whispered. "I don't know what you've done, but you've got to get out of here. Meet me at Pierre's Pizza on the corner in ten. Maybe I can help you."

She started to rise. I whispered. "The handcuffs."

"Oh, right."

Jazmin unlocked me and stood. I got up and tried to block my dimples with my hand, just in case any police were glancing in my direction. They're my most recognizable and beloved feature according to fans on the Joshua Mclintock website—both of them.

I watched as the police escorted several men out. I moved cautiously toward the door, trying to avoid being seen. They were busy so they didn't pay me any mind.

I raced outside.

It was dark now, so I wouldn't be too much of a target. I walked down the street looking for Pierre's Pizza. It seemed as if there was every kind of pizza place known to man—except for Pierre's. I passed Dominic's, Larry's, Habib's, Mid-Eastern, Mid-Western and Texas Tom's. Finally, I found it. The large white sign in front had a picture of a man tossing a pizza in the air. He wore a chef's hat, and had a toothy smile.

The windows were dirty and a small paper posted on them indicated that today you got five extra mushrooms on every slice. It was hard to believe there weren't lineups down the block for that.

I sauntered in, trying to look like a regular customer. There were six small wooden tables, but only one guy sitting down and eating. Behind the counter, a man in a white apron stood beside an oven. I assumed that was Pierre even thought he had more of a grimace than a toothy smile. In fact, I didn't see too many teeth. A potted plant stood in the corner looking like it needed some love.

"You want pizza?" Pierre asked with an accent that sounded more Italian than French.

"Uh, no, just waiting for someone."

"No waiting. Order or get out."

He was a master salesman. I had to go. I didn't have money to order a pizza and still have enough for my hotel room.

I headed toward the door when it opened and Jazmin

entered. She wore a blue blouse, tartan skirt and black hose. She looked different without all her makeup. Even more beautiful—if that was possible.

She smiled. "Take a seat."

I pointed to Pierre. "He won't, uh..."

She had already gone to the counter. "Hey, Pierre." She kissed him on the lips and he handed her pizza on a plate. Then he threw on some extra pepperonis.

"Thanks."

I'd always wondered what it took to get extra toppings. Although I didn't think I'd be resorting to Jazmin's technique unless the pizza guy was really cute.

She placed the pizza on a table and we both sat down.

"Go ahead, eat."

I grabbed a slice.

"I come here every day after work. It's the greatest pizza. Pierre's from Quebec. Apparently he comes from a long line of pizza makers."

I bit into it and was surprised at how delicious it tasted. Maybe that's why a lot of people became crooks. All the running and fear made you really appreciate a good pie. "Thanks for helping me."

"When I saw you, I knew you were in trouble. Not that a lot of guys who come to the club aren't. But I don't know, I got the impression you weren't used to that. I'm sensitive that way."

"You got a good eye."

"Guess it's from my acting training."

My eyebrows shot up like twin rockets. "You're an actress?"

"Used to be. Couldn't make it. Guess I wasn't good enough. That's when I went into strip...I mean dancing. I know it's really just stripping but it makes me feel better when I say I'm a dancer. I almost convince myself it's an art like ballet or jazz."

I looked at her and realized that she and I had a lot in common. We were both in the acting profession and I had once stripped at a bachelor party. That was in my drinking days when I would pretty well do anything for a buck. All the guys were really surprised when I took off the wig and bra. Well, actually, I guess they were disappointed. The lawsuit is still pending.

She chomped on a bit of pizza, and ate it like it was a sexual experience. "I hate actors now."

"Oh?" My shoulders tensed.

"So superficial. All they can talk about are auditions and movies they've been in. One track minds. I know. I dated one for three years." She took another bite of her slice. "So, what's your story?"

"Oh, uh, well..." I didn't really think it would be a good idea to tell her that I was an actor—even though I wasn't one of the superficial ones. I picked up a piece of pizza and coaxed my brain to come up with ideas. "I work as a telemarketer. Well, I did until last week."

"You were fired?"

"Not exactly. Someone got shot, but the police think I did it, and now they're after me."

"But you didn't do it, right?"

"No, of course not."

"That's what I thought. That's what all the guys who come to the club say too, even though most of them have been in prison a couple of times. She picked a pepperoni off her pizza and chewed it like she meant it.

"I really didn't do it. They found my watch beside the dead man's body. Someone must have planted it."

She nodded. "Uh huh. So, why aren't you in the slammer?"

"I ran. I had a, uh, meeting I couldn't miss."

"A meeting?"

"Amway. I'm this close to becoming a gold

distributor."

"Well, I gotta say that's an original excuse for running. I've heard them all."

"I have to prove my innocence." I debated whether I should tell her that the man I had supposedly killed seemed to look different to different people, but I didn't really think that would help my credibility much.

"So what's your plan?"

"I don't really have one. I figured I'd hide out in my hotel room for a while."

"Where you staying?"

"The Cameron."

She shook her head, her red hair bouncing all over the place. "I don't think that's a good idea."

"Not my first choice either, but with my present financial situation, it's all I can afford."

"No, I mean, the police probably know you're there. They never come into the club, even though it's a well-known hangout for criminals. I think they came looking for you."

"Someone's tracking me?"

"I think so. Why don't you stay with me for a few days?"

"Stay with you?"

"Yeah, till you figure out what to do."

I thought a moment. "Okay."

"I don't know why, but I kinda trust you." She leaned forward, her soft green eyes looking into my eyes. She spoke slowly. "Joshua, I want you..."

And there it was. The reason she was going to help me. I wasn't surprised. I guess telling her my story about the police being after me had gotten her all heated up. Danger did that to some women. Hey, that's okay by me. I gave her my George Clooney look—held my head to the side, smoothed my hair back. She was starting to say something else, but I put my finger on her lips. There was no need for words. Message received. "Sure, I can do the job, sexy." Then I gave her my patented Mclintock-slow-wink.

She pulled my fingers off her mouth and then pronouncing each word distinctly said, "I meant, I want you—to leave me a piece of pizza. You've eaten almost all the slices."

I looked down at the single piece of pizza left on the plate. "Oh, uh, sorry, guess I was hungry. Sure have it."

She ate the last slice, and I tried to recover my dignity.

We left and walked over to The Cameron together. She stayed in the lobby while I went to my room and grabbed my stuff. When I went back to the check-out with her, Smiley greeted me, showing off an even bigger grin than I'd seen before.

"I knew there'd be a woman."

"No, it's not like that...I'm leaving."

Suddenly, the smile drained from his face like some vampire had sucked it out. "You said you were going to have an extended stay."

"Uh, circumstances changed, I'm afraid."

He looked upset like he just lost his best friend. He even wiped his eye. I figured he was about to say something heart-warming like you'd find on a Hallmark card—like "May the world's blessings be upon you" or "Live long and prosper." Instead I got, "You owe me another twenty, buddy. I discounted your rate based on the fact that you were going to stay a few days."

"Look, I, uh..."

Jazmin moved close to Smiley and held his hand. "Mister, we're sorry, but this man has to see his mom in the hospital. She's on her last breath. Could go at any moment. Do you understand?"

The man started to shake. Probably the last time he'd been so close to a woman was 1942. He finally got words out. "Don't worry about the money. Come back anytime."

I had a hunch that message was mostly for Jazmin.

She kissed his cheek. His eyes lit up like he was a baby Venus Fly trap with its first kill.

We drove to her place which was only a couple of blocks down the street. She lived in a small apartment off Kingston Avenue. The furniture was simple, a two person couch, an Ikea coffee table and lots of animal photographs on the wall—mostly dogs and cats.

"Nice pictures."

"Thanks. They were my pets."

"Were?"

She gave me a sinister look. "Yeah, they all died mysterious deaths. Want some tea?"

Suddenly, I wasn't sure I wanted tea. "You like animals, right?"

"Just kidding. Actually, the only one that's mine is the poodle—Bucky. We were inseparable when I was ten. Then he passed on to that great dog park in the sky. At least now he can be off leash for eternity."

I nodded.

When she went to the other room to get some tea, I sat on her couch and picked up a binder that sat on the table. It was a book of photos from the various roles Jazmin had played over the years. There was young Jazmin as Tinker Bell in Peter Pan. Then there was older Jazmin playing a hooker in some TV drama. That's quite a jump.

There were hundreds of pictures. She had had the acting bug and yet she had given it all up. I started thinking about my career and the painful twists and turns it had taken, but I tried to force those thoughts out of my brain.

"Tea served." Jazmin entered carrying a gold tray with two cups. She sat down beside me on the couch and slid the tray onto the coffee table.

"Thanks again for helping me," I said.

"It's alright. I've been in some tough situations myself," she said, taking a sip of her tea. "When I was younger, I used to shoplift. Luckily, the cop who caught me put me straight and became like a mentor." She pointed toward my cup. "Try yours."

I'm not really a tea guy but I fell in love with this.

"Tastes like Blueberry."

She nodded. "Yeah, it's my favorite." She checked her watch. "Oh, the news is on." She turned on the TV and Jessica Thompson, a young blonde newscaster spoke.

"And police are still on the lookout for Joshua Mclintock."

I cringed.

"Recently it has been discovered that theatrical agent, Wallace Greg, who Mclintock killed a few days ago had ties to the mob."

Chapter Twenty-Four

My eyes were riveted to the screen as they showed my picture alongside a photo of Greg. The Greg whom Marty had described with the fatter face and lower eyebrows.

"Police are worried there is going to be a blood-bath as the other lieutenants in the organization try to locate Mclintock and bring him down. They believe he may have been hired by the notorious Delucca Crime Family to take out Greg."

My whole body trembled like the earth before a volcano erupts. "This is unbelievable. Now they think I'm a hit man."

Jazmin stared at me, her eyes wide open. "I thought this Greg guy was just a showbiz agent."

"Me too," I said, my body still trembling. "Now the police and the mob are both going to be after me. I'm so screwed."

"So let me get this straight. Greg was an agent but he was also a mob henchman."

"I guess. But then there's also the part about Greg looking different in different photos."

I could see her mind trying to make sense of it all, trying to piece this whole crazy business together. That would take a lot of piecing.

I stood up. "Look, I know I sound like I should be in the loony bin. But I'm not crazy." At that moment, it occurred to me that I had to tell her the whole truth. "I'm actually an actor, so maybe you shouldn't believe that part about my not being crazy."

She stared at me a moment. "That explains a lot."

"I didn't want to tell you after what you said about actors."

I spent the next twenty minutes giving her my resume. I tried to leave out the dead body roles as they tended to not impress people so much.

"That's a lot of stuff."

I nodded, trying to appear humble, a look that didn't come naturally to me. After that, we talked a bit more about my situation, while watching a movie where I analyzed the many acting mistakes that Ben Kingsley had made.

That night, I tried to sleep on Jazmin's couch, but my tensed-up body wouldn't allow it. I kept tossing and turning, dreaming about crazy agents and mobsters and for some reason, the time I appeared in that movie about the first gay people—*Adam and Adam.* I played Adam and also Adam. I've never been so attracted to myself.

Sometime in the middle of the night, I felt a hand on my shoulder. I jumped. In my half-awake state I thought that it might be Greg or one of his "mob friends." Actually, it was Jazmin. She took my hand and dragged me into her bedroom. Of course, she didn't have to drag all that much, I was pretty much a willing participant. And let us just say that after a few moments of her soft, sweet kisses, I forgot all about the mob and police and learned that wearing handcuffs could be a good thing.

I awoke the next morning with a smile on my face, but when I turned to look into Jazmin's sea-blue eyes, I realized she was gone.

I got dressed and went to the kitchen, starving. She was at the stove cooking bacon and eggs. "Morning, Deniro."

"Deniro?"

"Yeah, that's whose name you were yelling during our, uh...last night in bed."

"Oh? Sorry. It's..."

"I know Robert Deniro."

I nodded.

"I made you breakfast." She put the plate on the table and I sat down. "Thanks." I looked at my watch. "Uh, before I eat, I gotta call my agent."

"Yeah, I remember when I was obsessed with calling my agent."

"I'm not obsessed."

"No? How many times a day do you call him?"

"Uh, five, six."

She smiled and nodded as if that proved something.

I ignored her ten cent analysis and dialed his number. Jazmin was so wrong about me. I only called Biggie when absolutely necessary. And it was necessary sometimes to call your agent more than once, perhaps, on occasion, nine or ten times a day. Especially, if you had an audition and weren't sure if you should leave your sideburns the way they were, or shorten them half an inch. Or if you needed to know if you should wear your blue shirt with the stars or the red one with the cowboy pattern. "Hello, Biggie? Any new auditions?"

Biggie's voice was different—stern. "Joshua, don't you have bigger things to be worried about than acting right now? You're wanted for murder."

"It's all a big misunderstanding."

Biggie paused. Pauses were not good.

"I really should drop you as a client."

My heart stopped beating for a moment and I couldn't breath. In this town, without an agent you were dead meat.

"No, don't do that, Biggie. Everything will be fine in a few days. The papers just haven't gotten the news that

I'm an innocent man yet. Once that happens, I'll be a...a hero. Think of the great publicity then."

"You have till Friday to clear everything up or I'm going to have to release you from your contract."

I heard the click of the phone being hung up and I sat down feeling faint. Jazmin looked at me like she was staring into a Magic Eight Ball that wouldn't tell her the future. "What's wrong?"

"Something terrible. My agent is thinking of dropping me."

"That's what you're upset about? Did you ever think that maybe your priorities are screwed up?"

"The thing is, acting's the only thing I've loved that ever loved me back. Being in a movie or TV show or play gives me a special feeling that I don't get anywhere else."

She moved close and looked me in the eye. "In all the years you've been doing this, did you ever end up with that one big role?"

I was about to answer that, when someone buzzed the door. Probably a good thing because the answer would have made me even more depressed. Jazmin pushed the button on her intercom. "Hello, can I help you?"

"It's the police. Is this Jazmin Rogers?"

"Yes."

"Is Joshua Mclintock there?"

"Who?"

"Miss Rogers, he's a dangerous man. We need to come up there and take him into custody."

Jazmin looked over at me, thinking. "I don't know what you're talking about. I don't know any...what was his name again?"

At that moment, I realized that she was still a great actress. She whispered to me. "I have to let them up or they'll know something's going on."

"Buzz us up now or you'll be held as an accessory."

I knew I had to get out of there. Jazmin had been nothing but nice to me and I didn't want to see her get in any more trouble. "I'm leaving." I grabbed my bag which I hadn't even unpacked. I kissed Jazmin and thanked her for everything. As I left the front door, I heard her buzz the cops up. I ran down the back stairs, having no clue where to go next.

I walked down the street, keeping my head low so I wouldn't be noticed. That's not easy for an actor. We're born entertainers and all we want is to be seen by millions of people and hear their laughter and applause. Is that so much to ask? Of course, some affect a shy personality and say they're timid off-stage so it looks like they're a better actor when they're massively confident on stage. One American actor pretends to be Spanish in her real life so people are impressed when she suddenly speaks perfect English when she's on TV.

I never believed in that. I always thought you should be who you really are. But maybe that was wrong.

It had been a close call at Jazmin's apartment and I began to realize that maybe the dream was over. Biggie was threatening to get rid of me unless everything was cleared up by Friday. The police were trying to find me and so was the mob. The only people who weren't chasing me were the ones I wanted to chase me—fans. The thing is, I hadn't done anything wrong to have my life collapse in on me like this. Well, except run from the cops. My fanaticism to showbiz had ruined everything once again. I knew there were other things in life besides acting and I probably should have involved myself in a few of them. The problem was I had no clue what they were. The odd thing is that it had taken years for people in the industry to know me, but I had reached a much higher level of fame as a criminal in one week. Perhaps, I should have gone into the criminal arts rather than the theatrical arts. More room for advancement. You could go from getaway driver to robber to mob boss very quickly. And I'm sure there were good benefits. Maybe even dental!

Things started to become clearer in my mind and as much as I hated to admit it, perhaps it really was time to turn myself in. Maybe if I did, the cops would go gentle on me. Hopefully, they would listen patiently as I told them exactly what happened and then they'd realize the error of their ways. Of course, I've never seen that actually happen on any crime shows on TV and most times, things seemed to end in long jail sentences and torture. I didn't enjoy torture unless it involved a beautiful woman squeezing my nipples.

Still, if I didn't do this today, I'd be running for the rest of my life. And now that the mob was looking for me too, it might be better to be locked inside a cell for protection. I made a snap decision.

I headed down Chelsea Street and over to 53 Division.

The police station was an older dirty-brown brick building, in-between a cheese factory and an eatery advertising "Genuine Mexican Burritos." Good thinking on their part. Selling Fake Mexican Burritos could get you seven years to life.

I inhaled the cornucopia of smells and walked into 53 Division. I stood in front of a wooden counter that curved around in a circular shape. Behind the counter sat several officers at desks, talking on phones and working computers. On the wall off to the side, I saw photos of various policemen and the awards they had won. Even though I'd never won any big awards, I felt it would be a feather in my cap if I was arrested by a cop who had.

A burly officer with a round face sat at a desk near the front of the counter. He was reading the front page of the newspaper. Usually people with round faces smiled a lot. Not him. His face looked mean and hardened, probably from spending so much time around the criminal element and not using a toner and moisturizer.

I took a closer look at the paper he had on his desk. The headline read, "Still No Leads on Telemarketer Murderer." My picture appeared directly underneath it.

I figured this guy would know me instantly. In a way, I was looking forward to getting any kind of recognition. I hadn't been on stage lately and I hate to admit it, but I missed the attention.

He hefted himself up and walked over to me. He looked like he could do serious damage to someone. Exactly what you want in a policeman when you're being attacked by criminals, but not so much what you want when you are the criminal.

"Yes?" he said.

I blew out air and looked him straight in the eye. "Hi. I wanted to, uh, turn myself in."

Chapter Twenty-Five

As his patient lay on the couch talking about his childhood, Doctor Feldman's thoughts wandered. He'd been doing pretty well with Fitzgerald. His gambling debts had almost all been paid off. At least the old ones. The new debts, however, were piling up fast. He should never have bet on any horse named "Slow Leg McDonald," even if he thought Scottish horses were fast.

Why couldn't he just quit? Use some of his "mumbo jumbo" therapy on himself. He guessed the answer was that he just loved it too much.

"Do you think that means anything, Doctor?"

Doctor Feldman whipped his head around to look at Barney Robertson, the aging character actor who lay on his couch, his bright blue eyes staring at him.

"My dream. Do you think it means anything?"

"Yes, of course, everything means something."

"What?"

"Oh, uh, it clearly points out the conflicts you have within yourself."

A confused expression filled Barney's face. "Me being bitten by a ferret and the neighbor taking me to the hospital where I undergo fourteen hours of surgery on my big toe indicates that?"

"Yes. You won't allow yourself to feel these conflicted emotions because of the pain they would cause, so you transfer them to the ferret. The neighbor represents your other self trying to save you."

Barney stared at the doctor a moment, then an 'ah

ha' expression appeared on his face. "I understand, Doctor. It's so very clear now." His lips formed a big grin. "You are a genius."

Doctor Feldman smiled, thinking he was kind of a genius at this crap. "Tell me more about your dream."

As soon as the patient started speaking, Doctor Feldman began imagining what the 120 inch TV he was going to buy on the Home Shopping Network would look like in his living room.

Chapter Twenty-Six

There I'd said it. I'd confessed. It was over. I felt relief in the pit of my stomach. I could relax from here on in. No more procrastinating.

The cop's eyes drilled into mine. "Turn yourself in?"

"Yes. I'm the guy...you've probably heard about me, seen my picture in..." I would have finished that sentence, but my cell phone rang. I held up a well-manicured finger. "Excuse me a minute, Officer." I took out my phone. "Hello...oh, hi, Biggie. Yes, I know, two days till Friday. Actually that doesn't really matter any...what? They want me for that? Great, what time? Terrific."

I hung up, excited about life again. Some new theatre wanted me to audition for *Milk and Water*. It was an avant garde play that I had always loved. Biggie said they wanted me for the part of Water. Actually, I'd always seen myself as Milk. You know—frothy, bubbly. Still, it was work. That's what was important.

I put my phone away, happy. That is, until I looked at the puzzled officer in front of me and remembered where I was and what I had just done.

"You were saying you wanted to turn yourself in, sir?"

I looked at him, my mind working fast trying to figure out what to do. "Oh, uh, yes. I wanted to, uh, turn myself in...to a police officer."

"What?"

"You know, change careers, be on the force. How

would I do that?" Big smile.

"You want to be a police officer?"

"Yes, exactly."

He arched his eyebrows. "Oh, I thought you'd committed some terrible crime and wanted to confess." He laughed, his belly moving back and forth like it was doing the rumba.

I laughed along with him. Funny stuff.

Then his smile dissolved. "Didn't you say that I might have seen you somewhere?"

"Oh, uh, just that I'm around the area a lot, that's all."

He gave me the once over, and shook his head. "I'm afraid you're a little old to be an officer."

I was offended. I had taken care of myself, moisturized every morning, exfoliated at night, used deep cleansing masks. "Does it really show?"

"Yeah, it does."

This guy wouldn't give me a break. I didn't understand how he could be so cruel. I don't have any wrinkles. My hair was still soft and shimmery and my teeth were as white as a polar bear's butt. I don't smoke or drink and, to top it off, I worked out a week ago. God, what else did I have to do?

"We generally hire men and women in their twenties and thirties."

I shrugged. "Oh, well, that's that. See ya."

I turned away, glad to be walking out of this place. His harsh words had really wounded me. Just before I reached the door, however, I heard the officer's growly voice again.

"Just a minute; you do look familiar."

My heart started racing. I slowly turned back, covering the lower part of my face—you know, the dimples. "Don't think so."

"No, I'm sure I saw you somewhere."

"I don't really get out much." I looked at the clock on the wall. "Sorry, gotta run."

He rustled up his newspaper, then snapped his fingers. "I know."

My body froze.

"It was at the Morosco Theatre, a few weeks ago. My wife dragged me to a production of *Laughter in the Rain*."

My shoulders relaxed. I could breathe again. "Guilty...I mean guilty of being in the play, nothing else, clean record otherwise."

"I thought so," he smiled.

I basked in the pre-glow of his soon to be generous compliment. "Yes, I played, Henry." I tried to look humble, even though I personally felt it was possibly one of the greatest acting triumphs of the twentieth century.

"That's right, Henry," he said. "He was the drunk who comes on in the first act."

I must have made some impact on him since he remembered it so vividly. "Yes, you're correct."

He leaned forward, resting his arms on the wooden counter. "Worst night of theatre I've ever been to. My wife and I left after ten minutes. Couldn't get out of there fast enough."

This wasn't going exactly as I had hoped. He obviously wasn't the discerning theatre goer that I had pegged him to be. I had to get away from all this negativity. I looked at my watch. "Well, thanks for everything, Officer. Bye."

I dashed out of the station, got into my car and drove to the audition.

Okay, okay, I know I avoided turning myself in, yet again. Could you blame me? Even if I was going to surrender, would I do it to a guy who obviously didn't understand anything about the subtleties of acting? No way.

A few moments later, I landed in front of the building where the audition was to take place. It turned out to be an abandoned factory in an industrial area of town. It still had the sign "Zowie, the Wonder Cleaner" across the roof. I remembered the city had closed the building down due to the fact they were polluting the lake with chemicals. Officials began to get wise when local fishermen started catching trout with two heads. The Zowie lawyers contended that this was actually a benefit as that meant more fish for the consumer. Unfortunately, it didn't fly with the judge, who hated sea food.

There was only one other car in the parking lot. That seemed odd. Where were all the other people for the auditions? Maybe that was a good thing. Perhaps my résumé had so impressed them that they had already decided I was their man. No matter what, I was now extra-motivated to show that cruel cop, how great an actor I truly was. I was going to leave today with that part, one way or another. The only bad thing would be if no one else was here, and I still didn't get hired. That might screw my mind up for the rest of eternity and maybe longer.

I hadn't had time to prepare anything, but I had long ago memorized two pieces, so I'd be ready for any audition. One was from *Hamlet* and the other, *King Lear*. Last year, I'd performed the *King Lear* speech at a bachelor party. Those ruffians apparently didn't get the beauty in Shakespeare's melodious words and kept yelling, "bring out the babes." The guy in charge, a poetic soul, evidently hadn't told them that he'd used the "stripper money" he'd collected from them to hire a master thespian. Last I heard, his broken legs were still healing from those guys running over him with their car.

I walked toward the factory and turned the door knob. It wouldn't open. *That's odd*, I thought, and started banging with my fist. Nothing. After a few minutes, I kicked at the door. It creaked open and in front of me stood a tall man, with a wide face and broad nose. He wore a fedora-type hat, dark suit and what appeared to be Gucci loafers. He didn't look like the typical casting director.

"You the actor?"

"Yes, Joshua Mclintock. You are..."

He thought a moment. "Uh, Mr. Smith."

"Delighted to meet you."

I brought my hand forward to shake his, but he ignored it and started walking up the stairs.

I followed, neither one of us saying anything. When we reached the landing, we entered a small room with a chair, table and little else.

"Sit," he commanded.

I sat down and described my two prepared scenes. "Which would you like?"

He threw a scowl at me. "I'd like you to keep your trap zipped."

This guy was tough. But I decided I had to get something out into the open from the beginning. "Listen, I'm happy to play Water, but I have to warn you, I feel more spiritually in tune with Milk."

He stared at me a moment, then grimaced. "Right now, I'm thinking you're gonna play a dead guy." He started laughing in this high-pitched squeal that sounded like a pig just before being slaughtered.

I wasn't aware of any dead guy in the play. Perhaps, there had been a re-write. I must say I was disappointed. "Isn't there another role I could have? I mean, I've done a lot of dead guys; I'm up for a challenge."

"This time it'll be a little more real."

Chapter Twenty-Seven

The man began tying me to the chair.

"What are you doing?"

"Shut up."

"Yes, but..."

"I said, shut up."

It seemed rude at first, but then I got it. He was trying to get me into the scene. I've heard about some directors who inflict pain on their actors so that their work is more realistic. I knew about one who had been seared with a hot poker so that he could feel the agony of being burned to death during the Salem Witch Trials. He screamed so much, he got a mini-series out of it. I cleared my throat ready for the hellish sounds I was going to unleash.

I winked at Smith, indicating that I understood what he was doing.

He gave me a puzzled look, obviously still in character. After he finished, "hog-tying" me to the chair, he sat down, pulled out a cigar and puffed. I started to cough as I'm really allergic to cigar smoke.

"Can it."

Biggie must have mentioned my allergy to smoke. And now he was using it to make me really feel the character's hurt.

I tried to over-emphasize my pain by moving my eyebrows downward and making a snarly expression with my mouth. He didn't react so I pretended to expire. I closed my eyes and let my head fall to the side of the chair. I lingered in that position for a few moments. When I didn't hear a 'cut' or anything else from him, I asked, "How am I doing?"

He ignored me, just continued smoking his cigar. Something wasn't right. As I thought about all that had occurred, it suddenly dawned on me that maybe this guy wasn't a casting director after all.

Was this some kind of set up? Was Biggie involved? He was the one who told me about the audition. Or was it someone else? A moment later, I got my answer. The door sprang open and Livingstone, the agent who worked with Greg, sauntered into the room.

"Mr. Mclintock. We meet again."

"Yes, lovely to see you."

"Never got that script." He laughed.

"Still working on it."

"Well, you don't need to worry about that anymore, my friend."

"Why am I here?" I asked.

"I'm afraid you know too much."

"About what? I don't know anything."

"You've seen a few things that maybe you shouldn't have seen." He pulled out a gun, pointed it at my chest.

I had no idea what he was talking about, but it looked like it was going to be the end. They always talk about your life flashing before your eyes when you die. Nothing flashed. That's because I hadn't done anything. Oh sure, I'd appeared in a million small parts in movies, the theatre, and TV. But nothing major. Then I thought about my obituary—"Actor who played dead guys died today." Kind of fitting, I guess.

For some reason, Randy popped into my mind. Maybe because she was the only woman I had ever truly loved. Now, I'd never get another chance to make things right with her.

I looked at the gun, closed my eyes and waited for my final performance.

Chapter Twenty-Eight

Suddenly, the door flew open and a policeman marched in with a gun.

He was the same one I had seen this morning. He looked at Livingstone and his buddy, then at me. He put his gun away. "Good work, guys. You found him."

Livingstone looked at the officer, puzzled.

"You're undercover, right?"

Livingstone nodded. "Yes, undercover."

"Which division?"

He blinked fast. "Oh, uh, twenty-two."

"Twenty-two eh? Used to work there myself. Good unit." The policeman chuckled. "When did you find Mclintock?"

"Just now."

"Fantastic. Look, I know there's this rivalry between the divisions and all about who gets more lockups. But I just wanted to clarify that I saw the perp first. He came to the precinct, this morning. He wore some kind of clever disguise so I didn't recognize him. But then I saw the picture in the paper, and my cop instincts kicked in. I knew it was one and the same guy so I followed him here." The policeman smiled like he'd just been given an award as cop of the year, even though I had stood right in front of him at the station and he had no clue who I was.

He moved closer to the two men. "Look, guys, I realize I'm asking a lot here but I wondered if you could let me take him in. Twenty-two has all the good publicity they can handle what with solving the Dubois robbery last week. And the thing is, the Commissioner hasn't been too happy with us since we let that pyromaniac go and he ended up fire-bombing the Commissioner's summer home in Miami."

Livingstone's buddy stepped forward. "We, uh, did find him first."

Livingstone glared at him, gave him the hand signal to keep quiet.

"Look, I've asked you nicely, but I'm prepared to go over your head. I do know the chief on a personal basis." He took out a pen and pad. "What's your names?"

Livingstone's eyes opened wide, then he started waving his hands in the air. "No, no, you take him in. That's fine."

"I'm glad you see it my way. I'll even put a good word in for you guys."

"No need for that." Livingstone looked at the other man. "Come on, Fredericks; I believe we have some crooks to, uh, take down." The two men hurried out the door.

The officer untied me from the chair, then stuck a gun in my ribs. "Okay, let's go, scumbag. And don't try nothing." He escorted me out of the room and down the stairs. When we got outside, he pushed me into his car.

As the officer drove to 53 Division, I realized I'd never been so happy to be in police custody.

"Mclintock, you saved my bacon. The chief threatened to downsize us. But now, he'll see we run a tight ship over at 53. Might even get an award out of this. Perhaps a promotion."

"I'm innocent."

"Tell it to your mother."

"The evidence is all circumstantial."

"They found your watch at the scene of the crime. How much more clear does it have to be?"

"Yes, but no fingerprints, no footprints, nothing else."

He didn't answer me and didn't talk the rest of the way. When we got to the station, they took a mug shot. I tried to get them to let me apply a light coat of moisturizer as I was sure my eyes would show up puffy due to all the stress I'd been under. And what with the low lighting, I would look ghastly. But the photographer wouldn't go for it.

A few moments later, I was locked in a small, dark cell that smelled of death. One bed sat on either side of the room, the covers, a mess, on top of each. The guard told me I could make one call. I declined. What was the point? Everyone had pretty well abandoned me. Sure, I could phone Biggie, but I doubted he would come. He was trying to get rid of me and I didn't think calling from jail would help cement my image as a good citizen.

I sat on my hard-as-a-two-week-old-fruit-cake bed and decided to practice some of my voice exercises. You know to make me sound more resonant. I had the time. And maybe, just before I was granted my last meal, I could favor the guards with a little *King Lear*.

I pursed my lips together and tried to get an even tone. "MMMMMMMMMMMMMM.

MMMMMMMMMMMMMMMM.

MMMMMMMMMMMMMMMMMMM."

Suddenly, a shadow covered me and most of the room. Then I heard a low raspy voice. "Shut it."

I looked over and saw the biggest man I'd ever seen. He had risen up from under the covers on the other bed. His bald head was perfectly smooth and he had a large protruding forehead.

"Just doing some voice clearing."

"I said, shut it."

I began thinking that maybe my voice was clear

enough. "Sure, sure. I'll just go to sleep."

He grabbed my shirt at the collar, wrinkling it, and some of my skin. I decided not to hurt his feelings by saying anything.

"Yeah, go sleep."

I laid in my bed, but kept tossing and turning. Eventually, I started dreaming. It was a pretty good dream. They called me on stage to receive a Tony Award for my role in a play called *Prison Boy*. I started to thank the members of the theatrical community when Big Man suddenly appeared next to me, saying he deserved it more. He snapped my arms and legs like they were match sticks, then grabbed the award. At that point in the dream, the Tony changed into two pork sausages and I ate them. I guess I was hungry.

When morning came, I looked over at Big Man sleeping in his bed, remembered where I was and counted my limbs to make sure they were all there. Four, that's pretty good.

A few moments later, breakfast came and it looked delicious, if you're that way about burnt eggs, burnt toast and burnt jam on the side. How can they burn jam? I began eating and it wasn't half bad. I thought of it as Cajun style.

Big Man woke up and started eating too. He finished quickly, then walked over and grabbed my tray. I thought he might be trying to make amends for his moment of anger last night by giving it to the guard for me. "I'm not finished yet," I said.

"You finished." He walked back to his side of the room, eating what was left on my tray. He ate it up in about twenty seconds, then stomped back over to me. "Go time."

I raised an eyebrow. "I don't have to go. My bladder shuts down when it's stressed."

"Colin be here five minutes. You ready."

I tried to put together what he was saying in that Neanderthal lingo of his. "Someone's breaking you out?"

"Both us."

"Oh, that's very sweet that you included me in your escape plans. But I think I'm going to stay."

His face suddenly turned this red color that looked like pure anger. "You not stay. I don't want you tell cops about escape."

"The thing is, I'm innocent and if I leave it will look like I'm guilty. Do you get where I'm coming from?"

By his stony stare, I got the impression he didn't care where I was coming from. It didn't really matter anyway because a moment later, there was an explosion at the back wall of the cell. Big Man grabbed my hand like we were sweethearts, and the two of us scurried through the burnt hole. I'd never seen a man that big run so fast, everything wobbling like he was made of "Jello." We dashed over to an old Toyota that was parked in front. It had no fender, a shattered windshield and a dent on the door like a rhino had slammed into it.

Leaning against the vehicle was a black man in a white T-shirt and baseball cap. He looked pretty normal except that he only had one eye.

The even odder thing was that he got into the car on the driver's side.

Big Man pushed me into the back seat and yelled, "Go," to One Eye, who turned on the car and began driving.

I kinda thought that might not be a good idea, especially when he hit the fence surrounding the police station—twice.

I hated to be a backseat driver, but I said, "Maybe you should slow down a bit."

He ignored me and soon we were racing down the street at what seemed like warp speed. And when I say down the street, I actually mean in the middle of the street, straddling two lanes where the cars were going in both directions.

But I didn't have to worry about that for long because seconds later, the Toyota had gone off the road and we were driving on a grassy hill beside a cliff that had a seventy foot drop.

Then we were back on the road again. I leaned forward and spoke to Big Man, trying to keep the fear out of my voice. "Maybe you should drive."

Big Man glared at me. "He only one with license. Don't wanna break no laws." He started to laugh and One Eye joined in. Yeah, sure, it's funny until someone loses an...oh well, never mind.

One Eye turned toward me smiling. "Don't worry, I got glasses."

He did indeed have glasses on. It didn't really comfort me all that much. Especially since he was now looking at me, not the road. And three vehicles were coming toward us in the lane we were driving in.

"Cars coming!" I screamed.

He spun around, his eye now fully focused on the road. He swerved the car onto the grassy hill again, narrowly avoiding tumbling down the seventy foot drop where we would have been stuck for days and eventually eaten by bears.

"I good driver," One Eye said.

I didn't see how things could get much worse—that is until I heard the siren.

I looked in the rearview mirror and saw the reflection of a cop car.

We zig-zagged down several side streets, then made sharp turns, U-turns, screechy turns and every other possible turn you can make. Eventually, we didn't hear the siren any more. One Eye finally slowed down. We turned off onto a gravel road and drove past several farm houses. Eventually, we came to a wooden shack and One Eye parked in front. It looked like the kind of place a farmer would store his crops. Big Man left the car and pulled me out like he was grabbing meat from a freezer. We lumbered up the creaky steps into the shack.

It didn't look much better on the inside. There were a few chairs and a lamp on the table that I was surprised actually worked. He pushed me into one of the chairs and ordered One Eye to tie me up. Again with the tying up? This was unbelievable. Twice in one day, what's with that? On the other hand, I was starting to like it. If I lived through this, I might think about getting into bondage.

I only hoped One Eye's skills at tying up people weren't all that great. But he surprised me. After ten minutes, I was wrapped up like a Christmas present.

Chapter Twenty-Nine

Fitzgerald leaned back on the couch in his penthouse apartment. He was feeling the happiest he'd ever felt, except for that one time when his mom bought him Air Jordan's. Of course, the happiness was gone five minutes later when they were too large and he fell over and hit his head.

But today he had good news. Mclintock had finally been caught and put in jail. Thank goodness he wouldn't be in the papers all the time bringing attention to the operation. From now on, everything would be clear sailing.

Just then, his phone rang.

"Hello? Oh, hey, Carlos. What? Yeah, I just heard; he's been captured and won't be...What? Escaped? No, no, can't be. It is?" Fitzgerald felt his heart race and a tear beginning to form in his eye. "Okay, tell 'The Group' to meet me tonight. We have to take care of that nuisance once and for all."

Chapter Thirty

I looked down at my body and realized One Eye had tied my hands to my legs. Unusual tying procedure, but I found it in my heart to forgive him due to his ocular handicap.

My captors left me alone and walked into some other room.

To keep myself going, I performed *Hamlet* in my mind, but it really bothered me that I couldn't strike any of my usual grand theatrical gestures. This was the second worst punishment of my life. The first happened when I was seven and my parents sent me to my room without my Michael Caine *Acting in Film* videos.

Big Man appeared once again and said that they were debating what to do with me. He didn't exactly say it like that. He said something like, "Thinking what do you." A moment later, I figured he'd decided when he brought out a gun. But then One Eye came to my defense by saying that instead of shooting me, they should go out and have a few drinks. They could always shoot me later. Thank goodness for One Eye's strong moral code.

They left and I was alone in the shack. I looked around for something to untie the ropes. Unfortunately, there wasn't much. The floor was littered with garbage and on the table all I saw were their empty plates, some maple syrup, a piece of ham and a few forks. I figured I'd try to get to the forks and use them to untie myself. I forced the chair over to the table, slid my chest on it so that I could pull the silverware onto my lap. But all that happened was the container of maple syrup spilled all over my hands and the ham bounced onto the ground.

I sat there a while thinking what to do when I heard a knock at the door. Hope filled my heart. Someone had realized I was missing and had come to save me. But why were they knocking? Usually, the Police, Navy, Marines, the Power Rangers just pounded the door down.

Another knock. Actually, now that I thought about it, the sound was more like a bang. A moment later, I found out why. The door sprang open and an enormous animal clopped in. It was huge, and furry and angry-looking. After carefully examining its antlers, I cleverly deduced that it was a moose.

He blew out a cloud of breath, then his eyes hopped around the room for a moment, finally focusing on the slab of ham on the ground. He moved toward it and started eating. He seemed to enjoy tearing the ham apart as I'm sure he was going to enjoy tearing me apart very soon.

After about ten minutes, he had completed chomping down the meat and came toward me. I stared into his football-sized eyes. I guess my nervousness got the better of me and I accidently gave him the Mclintock-slow-wink. Not a good idea. He came toward me, nostrils flaring, passion written all over his face. He sniffed my hands, then his long wet tongue came out and began licking them.

I thought at first that love was in his heart, but was slightly disappointed when I realized it was probably the maple syrup. He seemed to think that the ropes were some kind of treat and began chewing them. As his teeth grinded on them, they began to fray. It was a close call now as to who was my greatest hero—Deniro or my moose.

Five minutes later, he stopped licking and I saw another look in his eye. I just hoped it wasn't the thought, "now, let's try mating with this beautiful creature." But he seemed to have completely lost interest and hustled through the open door.

That was good news for me. I could move my hands a bit and after a few hard pulls, the frayed ends of the ropes gave way. I hoped I had most of my digits left from the moose encounter, but I wasn't going to check that out now. I stood up and dashed out of the cabin.

Chapter Thirty-One

My first order of business was to figure out where the hell I was. I only knew it was Moose Country with a population that I had so far calculated as one. I headed toward the gravel road that we had taken to get here.

I stood by the road waiting for all the cars to stop. But there were no cars. The road was deserted. An old Pontiac did ramble down the road, but it just kept going. At times like this you wish you had a woman with you, who, like in the movies, could show off her legs, and get drivers to stop. Of course, she would later turn out to be a double agent who worked for the Russians and would then stick bamboo shoots under your fingernails until you revealed secrets of national security.

Finally, a dusty red truck with the name "Perry's Potatoes" appeared. I jumped up and down trying to get his attention. Finally, his brakes slammed. I raced over and he opened the door.

He was a grizzled-looking guy wearing a blue-checked shirt and cowboy hat.

"What cha want, son?"

"I'm trying to get to Leaside. You know where that is?"

The man nodded. "It's on the way. Hop aboard."

I climbed into the front seat and sat down, sitting on my hands, hoping he wouldn't smell maple syrup or moose on me.

"What's your name, son?"

"Joshua."

"Nice to meet ya. I'm Perry. Most folks call me Perry, the Potato Man. What you doing way up here? You look like a city boy. Got a cabin?"

"Yeah," I said, figuring simple was best.

"You like potatoes?"

I shrugged. "Yeah, sure."

"Spuds are my life. Sell 'em, eat 'em, use 'em as Christmas decorations." He reached into a paper bag, pulled out a raw potato, then proceeded to eat it like it was an apple. "Want one?"

I rubbed my stomach. "Trying to cut back."

He started telling me all about spuds, how they grow, the best way to cook them.

"I once found a potato that resembled President Abraham Lincoln. When you put that little top hat on him, you'd swear he was going to recite The Gettysburg Address."

As interesting as that story was, I started to fall asleep. I guess having had a full day with being in jail, taken as a hostage and then getting hit on by a moose, tired me out. When I awoke, Perry was still talking.

"...and that's how they got the name 'spuds.' Now, the name 'potato' comes from the..."

Suddenly, the brakes screeched and he came to a full stop.

"What happened?" I asked.

"We're here. Too bad. The potato story is a doozie."

"Yeah, that is too bad." I looked out the window and saw that we were now in front of Wigby's, Leaside's major department store. "Well, thanks for the lift."

"Gotcha," he said, taking another bite of his potato.

He left, bringing happiness to millions of spud lovers across the country.

I walked down Chestnut Street keeping my head down, knowing I had to be careful. I was sure my picture was in a few more papers by now, but I needed to see Biggie to ask him about that last audition where I was tied up and almost killed. Did he know what was going to happen?

I took a taxi to the Zowie factory and got my car from the empty lot. Then I headed over to Biggie's office.

I could tell, as usual, that Charlotte wasn't all that happy to see me. She stood up, showing off a short red skirt and her long delicious legs.

I gave her my sexiest growl. She looked at me a moment, then I saw the same fiery look in her eyes that I'd seen when we were going out. That was odd. Last time I'd talked to her, she didn't want anything to do with me. I guess my growls were more potent than I thought. Either that or she sensed that I was now a dangerous man. Women love danger. That's why I jay-walk so often. Gets them all fired up. "I have to ask you something Charlotte."

She growled back at me, now a big grin on her face. "Yes, I still have that leopard-skin bikini. I could wear it tonight."

She gently rubbed my trapezoids getting them all horny. "And I also have the peek-a-boo halter top." She smiled seductively, sat on the desk swinging those exquisite legs. I stepped away, trying to concentrate. I didn't get a chance to ask her about Biggie when the man himself came out of his office. His mind seemed to be elsewhere since he didn't seem to notice Charlotte's somewhat un-business-like behavior on the desk. He asked me to come into his office.

I got right to the point as soon as I sat down. "I have to ask you something, Biggie. Who set that last audition up? You know the one at the old Zowie Factory."

"A casting director I didn't know. Said he was aware of your work and that you'd be perfect for the part of Water."

"Biggie, there were two guys there and they tried to kill me. I was lucky I got arrested by the police."

He stared at me like I was an exhibit from the crazy house. "It's Friday, Joshua. I told you if you hadn't cleared this up by today, it was over between us. No one wants to deal with a fugitive."

My brain struggled to come up with reasons why he should keep me on. "I thought bad publicity helped a career. Look at the Kardashians. A sex tape, a fake marriage. They're making millions."

"Yeah, those kind of scandals work. But yours, involving a murder doesn't. He looked at me, his face morphing into a sad expression I'd never seen on him before. "Joshua, I can't represent you anymore. I have to release you from your contract."

My heart galloped like it was riding off into the sunset. Even though Biggie had lied to me and may have had a part in setting up that audition where I was almost killed, I didn't want to lose him as my agent. "But, Biggie..."

"Sorry."

He stood up, removed my picture from the wall and handed it to me.

"Good luck Joshua."

I left the office devastated.

As I slowly walked into the empty waiting room, Charlotte came over and growled again. "So, you want to come over tonight?"

I shook my head, no. I wasn't in mood for this now.

Her eyebrows clenched together almost looking like a uni-brow. "You're rejecting me again?"

"Charlotte, the other day Biggie sent me to an audition. Do you know the casting director who set it up?"

"You want a favor? Why the hell didn't you ask Biggie?"

"I did, but he said he didn't know the guy. I think he's upset with me right now."

She plopped down into her chair, gave me an annoyed look. "Maybe because you don't follow through on things."

"Can you check for me. Please?"

"Tell me why I should."

"Because it's a matter of life and death."

She stared at me a moment, then took a deep breath. She picked up a book on her desk. "It was Wednesday?"

"Yeah."

"Where?"

"The Zowie Factory."

She riffled a few pages, then looked at me like I was a Chinese puzzle. "That's odd; it's not here. This is where we record all the client auditions." She dropped the book onto the table. "The other thing is that that old building is hardly used anymore."

That hit me like a piano on the head. "Something very bad is going on and I think Biggie is involved."

"That's not possible. Biggie's the most honest person I know."

"You told me he meets Greg on Fridays. Is it on for tonight?"

"As far as I know."

"Thanks." I kissed her and though I don't think she wanted it to, a small smile slipped out.

I parked in the underground and waited for Biggie. Twenty minutes later, he came down the elevator, got into his Lexus and drove off. I followed. He headed south to Winter's Blvd, turned right on Ellis Avenue. Then he parked at 'Greek Town,' a small restaurant.

He walked in and that meant I had to go in too. I saw Biggie sitting at a table in the back with another man.

I took a table in front so they wouldn't notice me,

and ordered a coffee from the short, curly-haired waiter.

I continued to watch the men talk. A few moments later, the other man turned in my direction. I ducked down so he wouldn't see me. But I caught a glimpse of him.

It was Livingston.

I couldn't believe it. It was now clear to me that he and Biggie had set up that audition. The man I had trusted with my career had double-crossed me and tried to have me killed.

I needed to know what they were talking about. I called over the waiter.

"What would you like?"

"Actually, I wanted to ask you something."

"Yes, the fish is fresh." He came close to me and whispered, "Don't order the meatloaf."

"Actually, I need your help."

I didn't have any money to give him so I pulled out my wallet and removed the fake sheriff's card that I had used in the movie *Sheriff Town*. Everyone in town was a sheriff but the problem was there were no crooks. So some of the sheriffs began committing crimes to give them something to do. Then there were no sheriffs.

"I'm Frank Stalwart." I flashed the card. "I need you to help me on a case."

"A case? Wow. I always wanted to be in law enforcement."

"Those men over there," I said, pointing to Biggie's table. "I need you to tell me what they're talking about."

He nodded. "Sure, no problem." He gave me a smile. "Am I, like, your deputy?"

"Yeah, sure. Don't let them see you listening."

A moment later, he walked over to the coffee station near where Biggie and Livingstone sat. He moved cups and the percolator around, but I figured he was trying to listen. I thought I saw Biggie glance in my direction, so I quickly turned my head away.

"'The Onion Man'."

I looked up and saw the waiter standing in front of me. "They were talking about some guy called 'The Onion Man.'"

"You're sure?"

"Yeah. I got the impression that he was very powerful and that they had to watch their back."

"Thanks."

A few moments later, the two men got up and left the restaurant.

They both got into their own cars and I had to decide who to follow. I decided to go with Biggie. I had to know what was up with him.

He merged onto the freeway and headed north toward Belonia, a small area that was known for winning the world's biggest pumpkin contest—although there wasn't much competition and the winning pumpkin was only six inches high.

Biggie ended up at Arlington Heights Cemetery. He fiddled with the small electrical box on the side of the gates and they opened. He drove inside. I parked my car on the street and walked toward the cemetery. Biggie was leaning against his car in front of a grassy area where there were no tombstones. I found a hiding place behind some of the lovely flora that they plant in cemeteries so you don't remember that the ground has lots of dead people in it.

A few moments later, Livingstone arrived. He got out of his car, followed by a woman wearing jeans and a T-shirt.

Biggie opened up the trunk and took out three shovels.

They all began digging.

Chapter Thirty-Two

Dr. Feldman stared at Fitzgerald sitting across from his desk. Why did he always smell of meatballs?

He also wondered what was in that briefcase. He hoped it was money, as Tony had been threatening him again.

"I have another job for you."

"What kind of job?"

"Have you heard about Mclintock?"

"The telemarketer-killer?"

"Uh huh. The thing is he was a patient of ours at the lab and he escaped. We need to make sure he's captured and gets, you know, the proper treatment." Fitzgerald thought the proper treatment was a bullet through his head, but thought the doctor might not agree with his prognosis.

"What can I do?"

Fitzgerald smiled. "Well, it seems as if the authorities don't understand how dangerous the man is. If they did, they would have caught him by now. So we want you to do a couple of radio interviews and make sure everyone knows that he' crazy."

"I couldn't do that. I don't know enough about Mclintock."

Fitzgerald nodded, then opened up the briefcase. Dr. Feldman sighed when he saw that instead of cash, the briefcase only held a police file with a short two-page information sheet. He examined it closely.

"Now, your first interview is on..."

"Hold it; I haven't said 'yes,' yet."

Fitzgerald gave him a steely gaze. "I'd suggest you say, 'Yes,' if you know what's good for you."

Chapter Thirty-Three

Why was my ex-agent digging a grave?

I watched for what seemed like forever until they dropped their shovels and plopped down onto the ground exhausted. After a few moments of rest, they walked over to the trunk of one of the cars and lifted out a casket. From the trunk of another car, they pulled a body. A body! I started trembling. The body was placed into the casket, then carried over to the hole and heaved in. They covered it with dirt, then got into their cars and sped out of the cemetery.

I sprinted over to the grave to find out who they had buried. I wasn't thrilled to be that close to a real dead body. I didn't like being that near some live ones, but I had to know who was buried there. I began using my hands to dig out the earth, dog-paddle style. After ten minutes, I was exhausted, but I had reached the casket. I grabbed the top and began pulling it open. I looked down, but my eyes were suddenly bathed in bright lights and I couldn't make out whose body it was. I slammed the lid back onto the casket and waited. A moment later, lights shut off and I saw that they had been from a station wagon with the words, 'Arlington Heights Cemetery' on the door. I had to get out of there. I'm sure there was some unwritten rule about digging up bodies. Maybe a written one too.

The man in the station wagon didn't seem to notice me and went inside the office. I left and raced out of the cemetery to my car.

I sat in the front seat thinking, trying to figure out

what was going on. I had no clue. And who was this Onion Man? No clue on that either.

I knew what I had to do.

Twenty minutes later, I parked in front of The Moxie Diner. It looked the same as always. The outside was a bland gray color while inside, the walls were all yellows and golds. Also filling the walls were photos of celebrities, including mine. Which for some reason they had hung near the washroom, as if my photo was the reason that Moxie customers experienced gas.

The owner was a short man with a receding hairline named Phil Jenson. Before he started up the Moxie Dinner, he had been an ex con. Robbed a couple of banks. There were rumors that he had killed a man. I found that hard to believe. A man with such good table manners couldn't do something like that.

But if anyone knew who this Onion Man was, he would.

Phil limped over to my table and greeted me with a smile and the usual complimentary coffee which he always charged me for.

I tried as always to explain the concept to him. "Phil, if it's complimentary, I don't pay." Of course, he'd usually get all huffy and say, "then it's no longer complimentary."

Today, however, he ignored my comment. He leaned close and whispered in his always hoarse voice. "Didn't I read something about you being wanted for murder?"

"It's a mistake, Phil. I had nothing to do with it."

"No, I'm sure you didn't. Although I do remember you saying you'd kill that casting director who made you come three times for an audition and then didn't hire you. And you'd like to strangle that producer who threw you off the set on the second day of filming."

"Listen, Phil, if you're ever asked to be a character

witness for me, please say, 'no.'"

"Should you be walking around in public right now?"

"Probably not. But I have to find out who did the murder and clear my name."

"Any ideas?"

"The thing is I just saw Biggie burying a body in a cemetery."

"To someone like me, not actually in the profession, that doesn't seem like normal agent-like behavior. Of course, with the bad economy, people are doing all sorts of things to make a little extra green."

I glared at Phil, who didn't seem to be getting the point. "I don't think he's a part-time mortician, Phil. I think he or the guy he's working with killed someone and they had to get rid of the evidence."

"Who was the dead guy?"

I shrugged. "Phil, you ever heard of 'The Onion Man?'"

"Yeah, sure."

I stared at him, not expecting that quick of an answer. "You have?"

"Yeah. He supplies all the restaurateurs in the city with onions. He has a warehouse out on Denton Street. 134. Why do you want to know about him?"

"I don't see how it can be who I'm looking for. But Biggie and another man were talking about him. Said he was high up in the organization."

"And you think he might be connected to the dead body?"

I turned my hands palm up. "Maybe."

"I wouldn't put it past him. The guy's ruthless. You should see what he charges for Vidalias."

"What's his name?"

"All I know is 'Onion Man'."

"Thanks, Phil."

"No problem. And you know what? Forget about paying for the complimentary coffee."

"Great."

"Just pay the two dollar table rental fee."

I rolled my eyes. "Sure, Phil." Some things never change.

I left Phil and headed down to Denton Street where I saw the enormous "Onion Man" sign above a large black and white bricked building.

I ambled inside and noticed bins and bins of onions. All different sizes and shapes with names like 'Pearl' and 'Red' and 'Egyptian.'

I asked the glasses-wearing clerk if I could speak to 'The Onion Man.' His hand started shaking.

"Is...h...h...he expecting...you?"

"No."

"He...he...he...likes...a...a...appointments."

"I need to see him now."

His whole body seemed to tense up. He gave me a stiff nod, then walked over to a door. He pulled it open and the two of us travelled down a long hallway to an office, marked, 'Keep Out.' We went inside. A tall man with crinkly eyes and long combed back hair sat behind a desk, evaluating me. 'The Onion Man,' I assumed. He wore a blue shirt over his trim frame. His face had a boxy shape to it like he was a game show host. I expected him to tell me to spin a wheel so I could win some luggage and a home entertainment system.

"Mr. Oni...Oni...on Man, sir," the boy said, his voice trembling. "This man wanted to see you."

"About what?"

"I don't know."

"Geez. You have to ask what they want, Dominic. I've told you a thousand times. Ask."

"So...so...ry."

"Go."

Dominic raced out of there and The Onion Man pointed toward the white chair in front of his desk that was in the shape of an Egyptian Red. It squeaked.

"What do you want? One of the onions burnt your tongue? It got stuck in your throat? You got a rash all over your body? I've heard them all. But I warn you no matter whatever the lawsuit is, we'll fight it tooth and nail."

"No, nothing like that. I wanted to know how you're connected to a man named Biggie."

"Never heard of him."

"How about Livingstone?"

"Who are these guys?"

"Theatrical agents."

He shrugged. "The only connection I have to showbiz is that my son, who can't act, can't sing, can't dance and is allergic to water is somehow in the lead of an off-Broadway production of *Singing in the Rain*."

"Livingstone said the name, 'Onion Man' like you were someone they had to report back to, like there's some kind of mob connection."

"Hey, onions is a clean industry, not like those freaks at ketchup and relish. Now they have some seriously dirty laundry."

I stared at him a moment, pretty sure he had told me the truth. Great, another dead end. I thanked 'The Onion Man' and headed to my car, feeling hopeless. He seemed to have no connection to anyone or anything. And yet that was the name Livingstone had mentioned. I didn't get it.

Chapter Thirty-Four

As I walked to my car, I looked in an appliance store window. There were several TVs turned on. One of the screens showed Jessica Thompson, the newscaster. Behind her was a photo of an actor I knew. I couldn't hear what she said so I went inside and planted myself in front of one of the Sony Trinitrons that showed the same newscast.

"Noted TV actor Hiram Davies was killed today."

I shook my head in disbelief. We weren't friends, but I did know him.

Then Jessica spoke again and I heard something that made me feel worse.

"Apparently, killing-machine Joshua Mclintock has struck again."

Wonderful, just wonderful. Somebody killed Davies and everyone thought I did it. Of course, they would. Jessica continued talking. "It seems that Mclintock, besides being a telemarketer, is an actor as well. But not a successful one. He apparently played a lot of dead guys."

I stared at the screen, not believing what I was hearing. It was enough they said I killed a guy, did they have to pick now to share my résumé?

"What all this means, we don't know. To help us look into the mind of this killer, we have with us, Dr. Lucas Feldman, a psychiatrist who has worked with many showbiz personalities."

Feldman licked his large lips, smiled, then nodded.

"Do you think Mclintock is a psychopath, Doctor?"

"Absolutely. No doubt in my mind."

I cringed.

The doctor cleared his throat. "Now that we know Mclintock was trying to get ahead in the acting profession, everything fits together. First he kills Wallace Greg, an agent, then he shoots an actor. And not just any actor. This man was someone Mclintock probably hated because he was successful."

Jessica shifted some papers in her hand around. "But, doctor, the question I'm sure the public wants to know is why did Mclintock suddenly start murdering people? After all, before killing Wallace Greg, he apparently lived a clean life."

The doctor held up a long finger. "Yes, apparently. But there are many unsolved murders in the city. Who knows how many he's had a hand in." The doctor patted his beard, as if it were a dog. "A clear case of self-revenge."

"Self-revenge?"

"Yes, I believe Mclintock is punishing these people for he, himself, not making it in the industry. Yes, he's had some small parts, but as yet, he hasn't cracked the big time. Acting is all fantasy and at some point I supposed he got confused as to what's real and what's not. Of course, we all have these moments, but with his twisted, sick brain, it amplifies the confusion."

"So he snapped."

"Yes."

I felt nausea coming in waves. They had pinned another murder on me and were calling me sick and twisted. I stared frozen at the TV. Then I heard another voice. This one from behind me.

"It's great, isn't it?"

I responded without thinking. "Not really, I'm going to go to jail forever." Then, realizing what I'd just said, I turned around to face a man in a gray-checked jacket with a supernaturally big smile and teeth that a horse would be proud of.

"I mean, Mclintock is going to jail forever. Good riddance."

"Actually, I was talking about the TV. Isn't the screen amazing? 90,000 pixels. You can practically see the plastic surgery stitch marks on that news lady."

"Yes, it's wonderful, but at this point I'm just looking."

"Isn't that why we all want TVs? To look and see ourselves in the shows we watch. And maybe learn how to be better human beings in this great world of ours." Big horse smile.

Oh great, I got a member of the human potential movement-TV salesman.

"Wouldn't you like things to be this clear, this beautiful in your home? So that you could experience clarity and beauty in your own life."

"I have to go, uh, dentist."

"Sure. We all have our negative journeys before we reach our final destination." He took out a card with rainbows on it and handed it to me. "Call me anytime, day or night. I took the card and got the hell out of there before I was a member of the "Hari Krishna" or "The Children of God" cult and gave him all my worldly goods which right now was pretty much just the Max Factor under-eye moisturizer in my pocket. That area gets so dry.

He was definitely right. I was on a negative journey and not just because I had no beauty or clarity in my life. I was now on the freaking TV news. I have to admit, I did feel a little bit of pride. But underneath, I was scared as hell.

I left the store and, keeping my head down, ambled over to my car. My phone started ringing, but I waited till I was inside to answer it. Just in case.

"Hey, Jazmin. Great to hear from you." And it was. She was one of the few people on my side. She said she had something she wanted to talk to me about. Since the police were all over the place looking for yours truly, we decided to meet in the balcony at the Triumph Movie Theatre on Wagner Street.

It was an older theatre in the east section of Leaside. Grand and Majestic. They showed movies that had already had their first runs at the larger theatres. I may have had a bit of a hand in picking out the theatre as the place to meet. They were showing *Aliens on Fire* where I played the part of Domo, an alien species from the Planet Figlia.

I got my ticket and headed inside the theatre. There were only about five people in the balcony so it was easy to find her. The movie had already started and I was about to utter my historic line—"I can't marry you today. If the temperature goes down one more degree, I become highly combustible." But Jazmin distracted me by yelling, "Over here."

I let my annoyance go and sat down beside her. Then I proceeded to whisper about Biggie burying the body and 'The Onion Man.'

"Your agent is involved in this somehow?"

I shrugged, trying to hide my hurt. "Actually, he's my ex-agent now."

She looked at me and I guess she could see the pain. "He let you go?"

I nodded.

"You okay?"

"Not really, but with all that's happening, I can't process that right now."

"Who is this Onion Man?"

"I don't know how he's involved yet. Or even if he is. But everyone else is connected to the entertainment world so he doesn't really fit in."

"You sound like you're at a dead end."

"Yeah. What did you want to talk to me about?"

"It's Natalie. You saw her last time you were at the Lock Up."

"I remember." And I did. It's hard to forget someone who wore a beret and nothing else except Saran Wrap. That beret was very unusual.

"Anyway, she went on holiday for a few days and when she came back she looked somehow different. Her eyes seemed wider, something was off about her ears."

Jazmin looked at me, but I was watching my love scene with Princess Sabina, the half-woman, half-dolphin. "Oh, my God," I said a little too loudly.

"Yeah, I was surprised too."

"Not that. The movie; they cut out my scene. This is where I'm shocked that she isn't all woman. I had a rule about not dating sea mammals."

"Did you hear a word I said?"

I nodded vigorously. "I think we should go to The Lock Up and you can show me what you're talking about."

When we got to the club, it was nightmare-dark as usual. A woman, wearing a red outfit that looked like crepe paper danced on stage. Then she started tearing it off, piece by piece. I love arts and crafts.

"That's Cynthia," Jazmin said. "She's not the one."

"She's the one for me."

Jazmin gave me a playful slap. A few moments later, one of the servers, wearing the police outfit came over to our table. "Hey, Jaz." She was going to handcuff me when Jazmin grabbed her hand.

"He's with me, Roz."

"Angelo says every customer has to be locked up."

"You leave Angelo to me."

"Your funeral. What do you want?"

"Two cokes."

Roz nodded and left. Jazmin tapped me on the shoulder. "Natalie's next."

A few moments later, Natalie appeared on stage wearing a black evening gown. She did look different. Even the way she moved. Jazmin was right. She wasn't the same Natalie.

Chapter Thirty-Five

After Natalie finished her set, Jazmin wanted me to meet her, to see how she looked close up. She told me to wait at the stage door while she went to the dressing room to get Natalie.

A moment later, the two women appeared. Natalie wore a multicolored robe instead of the also very attractive...nothing, that she'd worn on stage.

"Joshua, this is Natalie," Jazmin said.

"Hi."

"Hi," she said back. Even with just that one word, I could tell there was something off about her. "Good show," I said.

Jazmin talked to her for a few more minutes, then Natalie went back to her dressing room.

When Jazmin returned, I suggested that we speak to her agent, thinking he might know something.

"Good Idea. She has the same agent as the rest of us. Pierce Modeling."

Ten minutes later, we were all sitting in Gene Pierce's small, but plush, modeling agency office. Pierce wore a checked-gray suit, black pants and dark blue Dockers on his feet. He had a receding hairline and a flat nose that looked like someone had tried to iron it.

He leaned back in his chair, looking relaxed. "What can I help you with?" he asked.

Jazmin's face turned serious. "It's about Natalie."

"Has something happened to her?"

"In a matter of speaking. She's been performing at the club. But she's different."

Pierce sat up and smiled. "She looks the same as always to me and I haven't had any complaints. As a matter of fact, she's doing better than ever. She got three new club gigs this week plus her acting career is taking off."

I raised my eyebrows. "She's an actress too?"

"Yeah. That's really what she wants to do. The stripping was always just a way to make an easy buck."

I stood up. "Look, I saw her too and there's something odd going on."

Pierce shrugged. "I'll check into it."

Jazmin smiled. "Thanks, Gene, I appreciate it."

Once we were outside of his office, I told Jazmin that Pierce wouldn't check into it. He was lying.

Chapter Thirty-Six

Jazmin crinkled her forehead. "You think Pierce is lying?"

"Uh huh."

"It seems you think everybody is lying. You told me the same thing about Biggie. Are you sure it's not you who's got the problem?"

"He knows something. When you said Natalie was different, he said she looks the same as always. You didn't mention anything about how she looked. You could have been talking about her personality."

"It was a slip of the tongue. Pierce has been my agent for four years. He's not a liar."

"I beg to differ."

"Well, you're wrong."

I'm very perceptive, Jaz."

"Yeah, very perceptive for someone who's been in the acting business all his life and doesn't realize he's going nowhere."

I felt a sick feeling bubbling up in my stomach.

She looked at me a moment, the kindness returning to her face. "I didn't mean that. But I gotta go."

"Please stay, Jazmin. I need your help."

She didn't answer, just walked away.

I blew out air, shook my head. You just can't win with women. Actually, most of the time I don't want to win. I just want to place or show.

That night I stopped off at a hardware store and picked up a shovel. I waited till after eleven, then headed toward the cemetery. I had to know who was buried there. When I reached the gate, I fiddled with the button on the box like Biggie had done and the gate opened. Then I ambled over to the place where I'd seen them bury the body.

There were numerous headstones in the area, but I found the spot where the earth had been freshly turned over.

It was spooky being there so late amongst all the dead. It felt like that night I stayed at the wax museum pretending I was a wax figure of myself.

I took a deep breath and began digging. It wasn't easy work and sweat streamed down my forehead. Several times I had to stop, sit down and recite a little *Hamlet* to get my energy going again. I really nailed Hamlet's soliloquy to Polonius and expected a standing ovation. But maybe not with this crowd.

I continued digging a little more and then finally saw the edges of the wooden casket. I dusted the dirt off the top and this time when I opened it up, I saw who it was. I stifled a scream.

Marty. My friend, Marty. I couldn't believe it. My dear friend was dead. But how? Why? I didn't know. All I could do now was bury him again—if I had the strength to do it. I closed the casket and began covering it up with dirt. When I finished, I looked down at the ground still feeling horrible.

But I didn't have time to think about that now because the next thing I knew, shots flew through the air like it was duck hunting season and I was a mallard.

I looked toward the entrance of the cemetery and saw a cop leaning against his car firing. I hid behind some trees.

I didn't think he could see where I was, but he must have, because he started running toward me. I dashed behind another tree. The cop started firing at the first tree, thinking I was still there. I took that moment to run through the front gates and out onto the street.

I kept running, not knowing if the cop was chasing me or not. After a few moments, my energy started sagging and I felt like I was going to faint. But I knew I had to keep going. The cop would realize I had left the cemetery in minutes.

I had to hide.

But where?

I saw a store and dashed inside.

The sleepy guy at the counter gave me a nod. "Hey buddy."

I actually didn't know what place I'd run into till I saw tons of DVDs on the tables and shelves. On a table was a huge pile of *Lassie, Come Home* videos for ninety-nine cents. I felt sorry for that dog. Spends his whole life in showbiz and it comes down to being sold on a discount table for under a buck.

I figured I'd stay here a few minutes to recover, and then be on my way.

Seconds later, however, I heard the door spring open. I immediately covered my face (mostly my dimples) with my hands.

I worried that it might be the cop, but it turned out to be a woman and a man kissing passionately. My heart started to calm down. Then I noticed the man was about twenty-five and the woman was...Edith!!!

I didn't have too much time to be surprised when she came to the back of the store sans boy-toy.

"Joshua?" she said, her eyes blinking wildly. "What are you doing here?"

"Here? Oh, uh, I was being chased by some, uh, autograph seekers and just popped in."

"Uh huh."

"And you?"

She shrugged. "It's a video store. I came to get videos, of course."

"Didn't I just see you kissing that 'toddler' over there in the horror section?"

Her face turned radish-red. "I, uh..."

"Does Randy know she's going to have a new daddy?"

She scowled. "Doesn't matter."

"Wasn't she upset that the last guy you went out with was two years younger?"

"She'll understand. She's going out with someone herself." She smiled a snarky smile. "Someone who's not a loser."

"Oh? How long have they been going out?"

"A few weeks, but it's serious."

I nodded, feeling that pain in my stomach returning.

"You had your chance. Screwed it up like you've screwed everything else up in your life."

That hurt. It was basically true, but I didn't need to hear it from her.

She didn't say goodbye, just turned around to head out. She walked a few steps, then turned back toward me, probably to remind me one more time how much of a loser I was.

"If you run into Randy, don't tell her you saw me here with...uh him. I can make things very bad for you."

I nodded, knowing she could. I was surprised that what really bothered me was that Randy was seeing someone new. I guess those feelings for an ex never really go away.

She left and I realized that it was time to get out of there. But, as I headed toward the door, it opened, and the cop who had been chasing me, stepped inside. I stayed where I was and watched him as he talked to the guy at the counter. Then he looked in my direction.

He pulled out his gun and walked toward me. I was cornered. There was no way out.

Or was there?

I grabbed a copy of *Lassie* off the table and flung it at him. It hit his gun dead on and knocked it out of his hand. Unfortunately, it didn't stop him from coming after me.

I grabbed more and more of the DVD's and threw them at him, two at a time. One got him on the head and he wavered back and forth. I used that moment to hurl more of them at him as I raced out the door. At least Lassie found some purpose in her later years.

Chapter Thirty-Seven

I ran around the corner, then back to my car. I drove fast and eventually ended up on a side street, hoping the cop wasn't still on my tail. I parked and headed over to 14 Reynolds Drive.

I knocked and an older man with a big smile greeted me.

"Hey, Joshua, how are you doing?"

I didn't answer the question, knowing that anything I said couldn't make what I've been through comprehensible. "I have bad news."

"Marty's not here right now."

I nodded. "I know. The thing is he's...dead."

"What?"

I wiped my eyes. "I'm sorry, Mr. Thomas. But Marty is gone."

"That's not possible. I just saw him this morning and..."

"He's buried at Arlington Heights Cemetery."

"Buried? How? What...?"

"I don't know, Fred. But there's something strange going on. I promise I'll find out what it is."

He nodded, unable to speak.

I told Fred that I'd arrange a service for Marty. He asked if I could say a few words. He didn't think he'd be able to talk.

Later that evening, I explained to the people at Arlington that a terrible mistake had been made and Marty had been buried without a service. They were very apologetic and said they'd fix things for Friday.

I went to a coffee shop and started working on a speech. I must have written about a thirty drafts. I wanted it to be perfect.

The next day, a small group of mourners stood around Marty's grave. Mr. Thomas gave me a hug and thanked me for being Marty's friend. "Marty always said what a terrific guy you were."

I shrugged. "Marty was pretty great too."

He nodded. I sat down and listened to everyone talk about him. How he was nice to older people, gave up his seat on the bus to the elderly all the time, and how kids loved him. I always wondered why the good had to die young. I hadn't led such an exemplary life, yet so far I was still kicking.

When it was time for me to speak, I took the wrinkled papers out of my pocket, as I walked to the podium. I opened the pages up and looked at the words I'd written. Five pages talking about what a great guy Marty was. In my heart I know it was useless to read it. I had to speak from my heart. I crumpled the pages up and dropped them back into my pocket.

"Marty was my friend," I said, starting to choke up. "And he was a great one. We're both actors so we had that in common. He would often call me if there was a part that he thought I might be right for. In fact, on a couple of occasions, he turned down something because he thought it might better suit me. Others have already spoken about how special a person he was. I just want to say that he was that and more. And I really miss him." I felt tears begin to fall down my cheek so I knew it was time to leave.

I said goodbye to Marty's dad and told him if he needed anything to call.

I got in my car and as I drove, memories of Marty danced in my brain. I thought about the first movie we had worked on together—*The Sasquatch Brothers*. We played siblings who lived in Orchardville. The town was in financial jeopardy so the brothers put on costumes and pretended to be Sasquatches. They figured that would get the tourists flocking to Orchardville. People came, but there was so much jealousy between the brothers that they ended up having a big fight, ripping off each other's costumes. When the town saw me, as the older brother, wearing yellow leotards underneath the fur, they suspected something was up.

The difference between real life and the movie was that Marty and I were never jealous of one another.

Playing Dead Man #3 wasn't what either one of us hoped to do with our lives, but now Marty's chances were gone and he was a dead man for real.

I left and drove over to The Moxie Diner. I sat down in my usual seat.

Phil limped over to my table. "Do you want a complimentary coffee? I've lowered the prices. A dollar ninety-five."

"Yeah, sure."

"You seem down, Josh. Something wrong?"

"It's Marty. He's...dead."

"Dead?"

I nodded. "His dad and I just buried him at Arlington Heights Cemetery.

"How?"

"I don't know. But remember I told you about the body that Biggie buried? It was Marty."

Phil's eyes opened wide. "He killed one of his own clients?"

I shrugged. "I don't know."

"That can't be right. He makes money from Marty, so he'd want to keep him alive."

"Sure. The thing is he doesn't make that much from guys like me and Marty. He makes the big money from his more well-known clients."

"I still don't believe he'd actually kill someone. That'd be like me killing someone just cause he wouldn't pay the complimentary coffee fee." He gave me an intense stare that made me think those rumors about Phil killing someone weren't just rumors.

I paid the dollar ninety-five and left quickly.

I walked over to my car, planning to sit for a bit and listen to some music. Sometimes that helps me figure things out.

But as I opened the door, I felt a gun in my back.

I could see by the car's mirror that it was the same policeman from the video store.

"Close the door, Mclintock."

I closed it.

"Now we're going to walk over to that alley beside the bakery. Don't try anything or I'll shoot you right here."

I did as he said.

When we reached the alley, there was a brown-haired man with two kids looking in a toy store window.

"Excuse me, sir," I said.

The cop whispered. "You're dead, Mclintock."

He wouldn't shoot me now, not with innocent people around.

I moved closer to the brown-haired man. "Sir, this officer would like a word with you."

The man smiled, came over to the cop. "Yes?"

I chose that moment to dash down the street.

The policeman screamed, "Hold it, Mclintock! I'll shoot."

I kept running, figuring I was safe. But then I heard gunfire. Guess I was wrong about that being safe thing.

I kept running.

A moment later, I heard footsteps behind me.

My only hope was to make it to Markdale Park and lose myself in the forest area behind it. Every part of my body ached, but I forced my legs to keep moving.

I turned the corner and sprinted down the grassy hill of the park. I passed several picnickers, running over, I believe, a chicken salad sandwich on white bread. Finally, I made it into the forest. Seconds later, I heard footsteps and shots again.

I fell to the ground.

Chapter Thirty-Eight

Fitzgerald sat on the park bench smoking a Cohiba cigar. The tension had left his shoulders and he felt reinvigorated. It happened when he'd gotten word that Mclintock had been shot. Finally, an end to this madness. He had been putting the whole operation in danger. But now everything would go down as smoothly as one of Figaro's meatballs. He laughed until one of the meatballs he had had this morning started to come up and he began choking.

Chapter Thirty-Nine

I felt a hand grab my shoulder. My eyes blinked, then opened completely. I stared at the out-of-focus two-headed furry monster in front of me. I screamed. It talked but I couldn't make out a word.

The monster head split and I now clearly saw it was actually two long-haired men with white beards. They were tan, their skin sallow. The clothes they wore were rumpled and torn.

Behind them, I saw a bald man who looked like he shopped at the same dollar store.

The voice came again. I understood it this time. "You awake, White Arm?" I didn't have a clue what they were talking about. But then I saw my arm, now all bandaged, and realized "White Arm" was me.

"Yeah, I'm awake. Where am I?"

He didn't answer, just lifted me from the ground and sat me on a large bolder.

One of the bearded wonders spoke. "You're in the forest behind Markdale Park. We live here."

"You're homeless?"

"A man is never homeless if he has friends." He smiled, showing nice teeth except for the black one in front.

"This is our home." he said, pointing to the forest.

"How'd I get here?"

"We saw you being chased by Harris. We grabbed you before he could get another shot in."

"Who's Harris?"

The other bearded guy stumbled up to me and stuck

his face in mine. An angry face. "Bad Man. Bad Cop." He spit on the ground.

The first man spoke. "Calm down, Blackie; this guy ain't got nothing to do with Harris."

Blackie sat down on the grass, pouting as if his prom date had just danced with another boy.

I looked down at myself. My clothes were ripped and there were a few blood stains here and there. I guess I kinda fit in with these guys. I examined my arm again. It had been wrapped up and taped like it had been done by a doctor. "Who did this?"

"Nurse Janis comes out to see us every few weeks. You're lucky cause she came a couple days back and fixed you all up."

"How long have I been here?"

"Three days. But most of that time you were kinda out of it. Kept on babbling about auditions and something about not getting nineteen cents."

I couldn't believe I'd been out that long.

"Let me introduce the guys to you. I'm Shorty, cause I'm short." He then pointed to the spitter. "That's Blackie cause of his tan and black heads. Beside him is Skin Man cause he's bald."

I said "hi" to everyone, although I ducked when I spoke to Blackie.

"I'm betting you're hungry, White Arm." We're all heading out to the soup kitchen. Are you up to travelling?"

Soup kitchen? That didn't sound good. "No, I think I'll find another place to eat. I've got money." I patted my pants where my wallet should have been, but it was empty.

Someone had taken it. I didn't have that much in there, but there was something. "My wallet's gone."

They all looked at me and shrugged. I didn't know if one of them had taken it, but what could I do? With no money, I had to go to the soup kitchen if I wanted to eat.

We left the forest area, walked through the park and ended up on a dirt road. Shorty and Blackie walked alongside me. Skin Man had a bit of a leg problem and lagged behind.

The soup kitchen was located in an old red-bricked building that looked like it might have been a small night club at one time. There were many tables where shabbily dressed people of every nationality sat and ate. At the front of the room was a counter like in a butcher shop. Several people stood behind it handing out food. I supposed they were volunteers. In front of the counter slouched a long line of haggard-looking men and women.

I picked up my paper plate and cup and waited in line with the others. The line moved quickly, but as I approached the person dishing out the soup, my knees started to buckle. It was Randy!

I knew she volunteered. I just didn't think I'd ever be a recipient of her volunteer work. I looked down at my torn dirty clothes. I couldn't let her see me like this. She would think I was even more of a loser than I was. I was about to get the hell out of there, but then...

"Joshua?"

I looked at her puzzled face and smiled. "Hey, Randy."

"What's happened to you?"

I shrugged. "Nothing."

"Your clothes are torn and it looks like there's blood on them. Your arm has bandages all over it, and...you're at a soup kitchen."

"I can explain all this..."

"Not to mention that I just saw in the news yesterday that the police think you've killed more people."

"Oh, no. no. I'm fine. Everything's perfect. The

police thing is pretty well cleared up."

She seemed puzzled. "It is? It didn't seem like that from the TV."

"It takes a while for them to get the word out."

"But the clothes..."

"Oh, that. Well, I'm, uh, doing research for a part. I've got a movie role where I play a homeless man who solves crimes. Gonna be a block buster."

She stared at me, not seeming to believe a word I said.

Suddenly, someone behind me yelled, "Is this the food line or a dating service?"

"Sorry," she yelled back at the guy. Then she filled my cup with soup and said she'd talk to me later.

I nodded, continuing down the line getting my hash browns, green peas and tiny cupcake for desert. Then I sat at a table with the guys I'd come in with.

I ate in silence while they told me about the jobs they'd had. Shorty worked in a jewelry store until he was accused of stealing. Skin Man was in construction, but had to leave after a beam fell on his leg. Blackie used to be a greeter at Wal-Mart, but got fired due to anger issues. Apparently, there's some rule about biting customers.

I told them I was an actor.

They seemed impressed. I talked about some of my roles and by the end of the meal we were like old friends.

Later, after I finished the small cupcake, Randy came over and took me aside. "I don't know what's happened to you, Joshua, but here..." She slipped some money into my hand.

"It's for a role, Randy, really!"

"Yeah, I know. But, just in case." Then she kissed me on the cheek and left.

It was nice of her, but it was one more nail on the

coffin that was our relationship. I mourned that loss for a moment.

Seconds later, I had other things to be concerned about. The cop who I now knew as Harris, burst in through the front doors.

I thought he had plans to arrest me, but he didn't even look in my direction. Instead, Randy wrapped her arms around him and kissed him. The kind of kiss a murderer gives the governor after he sets him free.

I supposed Harris was Randy's new boyfriend. The one whom Edith had told me about. Suddenly, I got that bad feeling in my stomach again.

I held my head down and walked toward the door. Harris was busy kissing Randy and didn't notice. I went outside, and a few moments later, Shorty and the gang joined me.

We sauntered down the sidewalk for a few moments, then someone shouted, "Stop." I turned to see Harris running toward us.

I quickly hid behind Shorty, kept my head down, hoping he wouldn't see me.

Shorty glared at the cop. "What do you want, Harris?"

"What are you creeps doing here?"

"Nothing. We just came for the soup."

"Yeah, sure. Were you planning on stealing food?"

Skin Man started to move toward the cop. He looked like he might punch him. Shorty held him back.

Harris gave them a mean look. "I ought to haul the lot of you into jail. I still think you had something to do with the bank job on Chestnut Street."

Shorty's eyes got this intense look, almost like a crazy person. "I told you last week, we're clean."

The cop didn't say anything for a moment, then shifted gears. "Seen this guy?"

He brought out a picture from the newspaper.

A picture of me.

Shorty looked at it for a moment. My hands shook.

"No."

"You sure?"

Shorty and everyone else nodded, grunted out, "no's."

"Well, if you see him I'd be willing to give you some cash."

Shorty nodded, said, "Sounds good."

Harris left the photo with Shorty, then marched away.

Shorty turned to me, his expression stern. "We have to talk, White Arm."

Chapter Forty

When we got back to the forest, we all sat around a fire in a circle. I turned to Shorty sitting cross-legged next to me. "Thanks for not ratting me out."

"We stick together, White Arm. The world out there hasn't helped us much so we have to help one another. Besides, Harris is a bad cop. He had Skin Man jailed for a month on some trumped up charge. He even planted some drugs on Blackie and slapped him around trying to make him confess to something he didn't do."

I saw Blackie's face fill with hate.

Skin Man stood up, walked back and forth. "I tried to talk to Harris once, told him we never did nothing wrong. But he wouldn't listen."

My mind reeled, remembering the kiss between Harris and Randy. "I think my ex-wife is dating him."

They all stared at me for a moment, then Shorty shook his head. "You have to tell her he's a bad man."

He was right; I did have to tell her.

Shorty shifted gears. "I never asked you yet, figured you needed time to recover. But what did you do that Harris is looking for you?"

I told them what I'd been through, and they seemed to believe me.

That night we sat around the campfire singing Christmas songs, even though it was July. It kinda put me in the Christmas spirit. Although the next morning I was disappointed there were no presents.

It was time for me to go. The guys all shook my hand and wished me well. Blackie teared up, but said if

I needed any help they were there for me.

With the money Randy had given me, I hailed a cab and had him take me to my car. I drove over to Randy's house about to go in. Then I noticed a lot of cops parked in front. I figured they were waiting for me to return. I knew I wouldn't last ten minutes without being picked up so I kept driving. A few moments later, an idea hit me and I headed over to "Costumes Unlimited," on Lender Avenue.

I had often come here and rented outfits for auditions so that I would look more like the person I was supposed to be playing. Sometimes, it worked and they gave me the role. That's how I got to play the zombie in the movie *Zombie Accountant*. Who knew the undead were so good with figures?

When I stepped through the doors of the store, Morry Sims, the owner, greeted me by raising his bushy eyebrows. He looked the same as always—pale thin face and big ears. The good thing about Morry was that he never read the paper or watched TV so he wouldn't have heard of my troubles with the law.

"Joshua, heard you were having troubles with the law."

"I thought you don't read the paper or watch TV, Morry."

"Don't. Son-in-law gave me a radio. They're talking all about you."

"None of it's true, Morry."

"I know," he said, raising his eyebrows again.

"I need a costume."

"You in some play or somethin'?"

"Yeah."

"Well, I'm a little low on inventory right now, Joshua. I got that alien outfit you wore before, and a Celine Dionne number, but I don't think you got the legs for it. I also got a cop outfit. What'll it be?"

I thought the alien outfit might bring too much attention to me on the streets of Leaside. Also, I worried I might get taken to some research facility and my pride and joy examined like they did in that movie I did—*The Small Man from the Big Planet*. The more I thought about it, the more I realized that the cop outfit might be good. The police would never guess that one of their own was a fugitive. "I'll take the cop thing."

"Sure, sure." He pulled out the costume and I got him to give me a fake moustache. I went into the change room and tried the costume on. It was a pretty good fit. I paid Morry and left.

I walked down the street feeling different somehow. I guess it was the fact that I was on the good side of the law for a change. I stood straighter, felt like I could do anything. Maybe it was my imagination, but it seemed as if people on the street were looking at me with respect. I'd never felt that before.

The more I thought about it, the more I realized that this was a terrific disguise.

That is, until a real cop stood beside me.

Chapter Forty-One

I stared at the policeman for a moment, then knew what I had to do.

Run like hell.

Unfortunately, my genius plan didn't work out like I thought and the officer ran like hell after me.

I increased my speed, but I could tell by the sound of his footsteps that he was right behind me. I zigged, he zigged; I zagged, he zagged. After a few more minutes, I was exhausted from all the zigging and zagging and didn't know how much further I could go. I started to slow down and a moment later, the cop and I were moving alongside one another. I waited for his hand to grab me in some kind of death grip and say, "You're under arrest, creep." But he didn't. He merely puffed out the words, "Who we chasing?"

Puffing, myself, I said, "Chasing?" Then it clicked. He thought I was trying to catch someone. I stopped running and the cop stopped too. We looked at one another, both still breathing heavily for a moment, trying to regain our ability to speak in words humans of this planet could understand. Finally, I coughed up a phrase. "Oh, uh, this bad dude. He's...uh..."

His eyes got wide. "Was it the telemarketer, the one who murdered those men?"

I thought a moment. "Yes, the actor who the police believe murdered those men, but had absolutely nothing to do with it."

He stared at me. "I thought he was a telemarketer."

"No, no, actor. A really good one from what I

understand. And I'm pretty sure he's innocent."

He started to laugh. "Good one. I've heard he's as guilty as a dog with chicken feathers on his lips."

"No, I'm positive he's innocent."

He arched his eyebrows. "You got some inside info?"

And then I said it. I knew it was a mistake as soon as it flew out of my lips. "Cause I'm an actor and I can tell these things."

He stared a moment, looking me up and down. "You're an actor?"

I had to cover. "It's a, uh, hobby. You know, part-time."

He grabbed my shoulder. "Okay, buddy boy, your time for running is over."

He'd figured it out.

Believe me, I thought about trying to escape, but I was just too tired. So when he stuffed me into his cop car, I didn't offer any resistance.

If only I hadn't said anything about being an actor, he might never have known. I had once again ruined things for myself.

He drove to 32 Division, not saying a word. Once inside the station, he planted his hand on my back and pushed me down the hallway. We ended up in a large brightly-lit office. The name plate on the desk said, "Chief Henry Davidson." Well, at least the head man was going to be the one to put me away. That would give me some kind of prestige.

Davidson had been staring at some papers, but looked up when the two of us entered his office. He had a military bearing and was probably nearing sixty. His salt and pepper hair and vanilla-ice-cream-white moustache gave him a distinguished look and made me hungry.

I sat down on the chair in front of the desk, while the

other officer whispered something into the chief's ear. The chief grimaced and said, "A runner, eh?"

The officer whispered something else and left.

The chief stood up and paced back and forth a few times. "I don't know what it is with you guys running. You know we're going to get you eventually."

I nodded, knowing he was right.

"What's the big deal anyway?"

I stared at him puzzled. "Big deal?"

"Yeah, about appearing in the Policeman Benefit Show?"

"What?"

"Don't play dumb." He took a sheet of paper from the top of his desk and waved it in front of me. It read, "Actors Needed for Benefit."

"You can't tell me you didn't see it. It was posted all over the damn station."

"Well, uh..."

Davidson scrunched up the flyer like he hated it and threw it into the waste basket.

"What the hell's your name?"

He didn't know who I was so I was free to make up something. "Uh, Tim, Tim Fisher."

He lifted his bony frame onto the top of the desk and looked down at me. "Tim, I understand why most of the other guys don't want to do it. Probably think actors are wusses. But what I don't get is that you already perform. Why wouldn't you jump at the chance to be in a production?" He spread his hands. "Is it because it's my first year as director?"

"No, no..."

"Doesn't matter. To be blunt, I need you. The production is in trouble. Williams, the only good actor in the bunch, left last week."

So he wanted me, a known criminal, to be in a policeman show. Not quite the big role that could take me to the top, but still, it was an opportunity to perform again.

"Besides, the money we collect is going to help the kids at the hospital have a better Christmas. So what do you say?"

Kids, acting. I didn't have to think about it. "Sure."

His mouth formed something that was close to a smile. "I don't want to scare you, but, there is some dancing and singing in the show. Ever done any of that?"

"Yeah, I have." I had done some dancing, not a lot of singing. But I'd learned in this business you should always say, yes. Even if they ask if you've ever been a Siamese twin.

"Fantastic. The show's next week and we hold rehearsals tonight, Wednesday, Friday."

Things happened fast. That night I stood beside the chief inside an older theatre known as The Wilkenberg. He was wearing a Hawaiian shirt and white shorts. Not exactly the right look for someone with knees that had never seen the sun and looked like pipe cleaners.

There were four policemen wearing their uniforms standing beside one another on stage. I felt anxious about there being so much "cop," in the room and even more nervous when I realized that one of them was Harris.

Luckily, he paid no attention to me.

The chief rubbed one of his pale knees and spoke. "Okay, everyone, I want to introduce the newest member of our team, Tim."

The officers all muttered, hello.

"Okay," said the chief. "Let's start the opening number. Tim, you see if you can follow the dance moves. It might take a bit of time for you to get up to speed."

I nodded.

You could tell they'd never danced before. It was like watching pirates with wooden legs doing the cha cha. "Okay," said the chief. "Why don't you join them on stage, Tim."

I climbed up onto the platform and began copying their moves. Suddenly, my dance training kicked in and my legs started flying all over the stage without me even doing anything. The other cops watched, shock on their faces. I was amazed that my body remembered all this stuff. My mind, on the other hand was far away, dreaming as if I were on *Dancing with the Stars* and the star I was dancing with was me. Suddenly, my brain realized what my legs were doing and I stopped. "Sorry," I said.

The chief shook his head. "Nothing to be sorry about. That was amazing. Never seen anything like it. Okay, you're lead choreographer. Teach these guys some of those moves you just did."

I was surprised by the promotion, but happy. The chief left and I spent the rest of the evening working with the officers. It wasn't easy. Most of them had no sense of rhythm. I sometimes thought that if cops knew ballet, criminal take-downs would be much more graceful.

During our break, an attractive blonde woman with a red dress, sashayed into the auditorium. Harris gave her a long sensuous kiss. I didn't know who she was, but she was obviously not the person who sold him insurance. I guessed from this that Randy was not his only special someone. Maybe he had a lot of other some ones. So, in addition to having a two-step that made me violently ill, he was also a cheater.

Sure, I hadn't been the perfect husband to Randy. And although she may have thought that I cheated on her—and I did come close during our rough times—I never actually did. I smiled, I flirted, but that's all. I never wanted to hurt her.

When the break ended and the woman left, Harris marched over and gave me squinty eyes. "I saw you looking at my girlfriend, buddy. Don't do that again or the only dance you'll be doing is a one-legged waltz. Understand?"

"Sorry. I was just puzzled for a moment because I saw you with another girl last week."

"This one's my Tuesday night. The other is Thursday."

I felt bad for Randy. She didn't even rate a good day of the week like Saturday.

Harris went back on stage and I continued choreographing the moves of the policemen.

When rehearsal ended, I headed over to Randy's house, not worrying about being seen by the cops in the area. I had the policeman outfit on, along with the moustache so I'd be unrecognizable. I parked my car a block away so if any officers were still there they wouldn't notice I wasn't in a police car.

Randy answered the door, wearing a cerulean blue dress, showing off perfect cleavage that could probably hold Webster's Dictionary. The unabridged one.

"Joshua, what are you...?" Then, her eyes fell to my outfit. "Why are you dressed as a cop and why do you have a moustache? The last time I saw you, you looked homeless."

"It's a long story." A lot of people may say, "long story," but I meant it. "I need to talk to you."

"I don't know if that's a good idea. My boyfriend is a police officer and with your problems..."

"It's okay; I know Harris."

"You do?"

"Let's just say we're kind of working together."

"What?"

"Look, I came here to tell you that he's not a good

man."

She stared at me, her eyes not blinking. "What do you mean, not a good man?"

"He's a bad cop."

"That's not true."

"He's put people in jail for things they didn't do, planted drugs on them, beat them."

"He would never do anything like that."

I knew I had to get her emotionally. I leaned toward her and whispered, "He's done things to the homeless."

Her face twisted into an angry expression. "Why are you saying this?"

"There's one more thing you should know. He's seeing other women."

She looked as if she were about to slap me or kiss me. I would have preferred the kiss, but I had a feeling she was learning the other way.

"Oh, I know what this is about. You're jealous."

"It's not about that at all. I'm just telling you what I know."

"Look, Joshua, we had something that was good once, but it's over now and..."

At that moment, Edith popped into the room. "Oh, the loser is here."

I didn't need this now. I glared at her. "The police obviously don't think of me as a loser since they made me lead choreographer in their benefit show."

"Loser."

My anger was building. I turned to Randy and it slipped out. "Your mother is having a fling with a twenty-five year old."

Edith glared at me. "What are you talking about?" She moved her finger in a circle as she pointed toward her head, doing the universal sign for loony. "He's nuts."

Randy didn't say anything for a moment, then shot

me a look and yelled, "Get out of here! Get out. I don't want to ever see you again."

"But, Randy..."

"I said, get out."

I couldn't move for a moment. Then, I slowly turned away and left the house, realizing she meant it this time.

Chapter Forty-Two

I got in the car and drove. Just drove. A million thoughts raced through my head. Maybe it was over for her, but it would never be over for me. I would always love Randy.

On Wednesday evening, I headed back to the Wilkenburg and continued working with the policemen dancers. A few of them had really improved. Some still might be mistaken for a team of near-sighted horses, but maybe there'd be some equine fans in the crowd.

The next evening the show was on. You'd think an actor with my experience wouldn't be nervous. But all the acting books said you should have anxiety before a show otherwise you'd come off as flat or dull. I didn't think there was any chance of that since I was performing in front of a house full of cops who could send me to death row at any moment.

The show started off with a short skit about a man on a street corner talking to a cop, trying to get out of his parking ticket. He spent so much time on it, the cop arrested him for loitering. Of course, the officer didn't see that behind him, all the while, a thief was breaking into a bank. Hilarious. There were a couple more skits, then some musical numbers. We changed a song from *Chorus Line* titled "What I Did for Love," to "What I Did for Forensics."

Two men then carried an eight step staircase into the center of the stage. Time for my solo dance number— the big finish of the night. All the other policemen in the show gathered around me in a circle. They began tap dancing, but the spotlight shone on me.

The sweat poured down my forehead. I was frozen. I couldn't move. I had to talk myself down with those words of motivation my last jazz teacher had given me—"Dance, you idiot. Dance!"

And then I was off.

I began doing a few simple moves which evolved into the more complex ones like tapping up the stairs and down. Judging by the "oohs" and "awes," the audience was really with me. And I felt great being on stage again.

Everything was going well. But then it happened. My moustache fell off. I picked it up and quickly pressed it back under my nose.

I continued dancing, but something had changed. I could feel all the officers on stage and maybe the two hundred in the audience eyeing me. And I didn't feel that they were watching because they loved my reverse shuffle-hop-step.

Harris stared at me like a call girl focused on a guy in an Armani suit sitting alone at the bar.

He tapped over to me. He was violating my strict rule of not altering any choreography, but it didn't seem to bother him. He whispered. "I knew there was something funny about you. You're that Mclintock!" He grabbed my arm.

I whispered, "We're on stage. Make it part of the show."

He looked at the audience, then gave them a cheesy smile. Still holding my arm, we tap danced over to stage left. Unfortunately, he was still facing the crowd and didn't look where he was going. We hit another policeman who fell to the ground which caused two more policemen to topple over. With this mess, I didn't think I would put this particular job on my résumé.

I struggled out of Harris's grip and ran through the

opening in the curtain. I raced down the long hallway ending up at the stage door.

"Hey, Officer Tom," said Bernie, the always drunk stage doorman.

"Bye, Bernie," I replied, as I raced outside and onto the street. As I flew out the door, I could hear him say his usual, "I love you."

I got in my car and headed down Thirteenth Avenue, still panting from the run. I turned right onto Lancaster and just kept driving.

I took off my moustache and policeman cap, then unpinned the badge on my chest. I threw it all into the backseat. I now pretty well looked like I was wearing a normal black shirt, except for the epaulettes on the shoulders. I figured no one would notice them unless they were members of the epaulette appreciation society.

I didn't know why right then, but the thought popped into my head that it had been a week or so since I'd checked for any audition listings. I looked back and saw no one following me, so I parked and, keeping my head down, ran across the street to see if there were any stores that might have *Variety*.

There was no one out on the streets, so the chance of me being seen was slim.

Everything seemed fine.

Then a limo drove up in front of me and a man with a gun said to get in.

Chapter Forty-Three

I always dreamed a limo would show up to take me to the Oscars. But I wasn't sure this was the one to do it. Especially when the back door opened and I saw Giuseppe Delucca beckoning me inside. He was a mobster who had been in all the papers lately. Many of the articles suggested that he had been involved in a recent attempted hit on the Mayor. What would he want with me? Then I remembered that Greg had ties to the mob. I felt like I had to get into the limo, taking into account the gun he had pointed at my forehead.

I sat down in the back seat, next to Giuseppe and the limo took off.

He took the gun away, put it into his pocket. "Sorry, Mclintock. It's just that sometimes people need a little 'persuader'."

I turned to face this master of crime, thinking he looked just like he had in the paper—big bald head, blotchy complexion, and tiny ears. He wore a dark suit as if he were going to a funeral. I hoped it wasn't mine. "Hi," I said, smiling. "Nice to meet you." Sure, he stole, and had people murdered, but there was no reason not to be polite.

"Nice epaulettes."

Guess I was wrong about no one noticing. "Thanks."

He gave me a stern look. "You've been busy, Mclintock."

"Not so much. In the winter, I usually get roles in a few productions. But now, with the summer here, they've kind of dried up. I'm hoping near the end of the season, I'll be able to do some summer stock and maybe..."

He gave me a look that indicated he might not have been talking about show business. And that he might want to curtail the conversation I was making and, perhaps, if conditions were right, maybe stick something sharp into my back. So, I decided to change my answer. "Yeah, I have been busy."

"Curious as to why you took out Greg."

I let that sit for a moment before responding. "I didn't take Greg out."

"You had one of your men do it?"

"I don't have any men."

"You prefer to do the killings solo?"

"Yes. I mean no. I didn't kill anyone."

He stared at me a moment, then started laughing.

"Good one, Mclintock. Look, we ain't the cops. We have no issue with you taking him out. He was a bad apple if you know what I mean."

"Bad apple?"

"Yeah, tried to cut us out of some deals."

I thought this might be an opportunity to get some information. "Maybe you can help me out here. What did he have to do with the mob? I thought he was just a talent agent." I moved close to Giuseppe, let loose my hundred watt smile. "See I'm trying to prove my innocence and..."

"Innocence?" He started to laugh again. "You're quite the joker, Mclintock." He sniffed a few times. Obviously, he had allergy issues. But I certainly wasn't about to give him the name of my homeopath.

"Don't worry about that. Let me just say that you actually did us a favor. And you know, one good turn deserves another."

"I'm not sure what you mean."

"We got someone else we'd like you to kill."

My breathing stopped for a moment. When it came back, I said, "You know, that's not exactly what 'one good turn deserves another' means. The way it works is if I did you the favor of shooting Mr. Greg, then you should do a favor for me."

"Okay, then the favor is you get to kill someone else."

I looked at his bright blue eyes that seemed to say, "I'm going to reach inside your throat and pull out your liver." I responded with, "That's very thoughtful."

His face turned pomegranate-red and he turned his hands into fists. "See, this jerk did a terrible job taking pictures at my daughter April's wedding. They were way too dark and out of focus. Besides that, they made me look fat. I don't want to look fat. I'm on Atkins." I looked at his protruding stomach that seemed as if he had swallowed a bowling ball, and thought that maybe he was still eating a tad too many carbs. I decided not to mention it.

"The videos were a whole other story," he said. "This guy always shot his damn camera at the wrong times, like when Tosco and me were discussing how to take out the guy who made the birthday cake. You know he spelt 'Delucca' with two 'c's."

I thought a moment, not getting what the problem was. "You know 'Delucca' has two 'c's."

He gave me that look again. "If I say it don't have two 'c's, it don't. Got it?"

I nodded, didn't say anything else. Mostly because my throat was squeezed so tight with fear, I couldn't.

A moment later, the limo turned into the parking area of a small strip plaza. Giuseppe pointed toward a photography shop. "That's the place."

I looked and saw the sign, "Photography By Diesel" in orange neon. The posters in the window indicated that he was available for weddings, bar mitzvahs, and any other occasion.

"Listen, I'm sure he'd reshoot the wedding for you, no charge. I'd even talk to him for you."

He held up his hand, showing off a ring with a ruby in it.

"You know what this is?"

"A ring?"

"It's from a man who wanted to talk about an extension on the money he owed me." He leaned close, so close, I could feel his revolver making a dent in my spleen. "He doesn't have the ring now—or the finger it was on, for that matter. But he does have a nice cemetery plot at the bottom of Lake Bernard."

"Your point is?"

"My point is, sometimes it's too late for talk."

"Sure, cause you killed him."

He shrugged. "What choice did I have?"

"Not to kill him?"

"Right, no choice."

He reached into his pocket and removed a picture. "This is what Diesel looks like, so you don't accidentally shoot a customer or nothing." He laughed, his belly moving like it was a trampoline with the entire Cubs Baseball team jumping up and down on it.

He handed me a colt forty-five. "Unregistered gun. I know you probably got lots of these hanging around in your arsenal. But I figured I'd make it a bit easier for you." In my other hand he placed a roll of bills. "And here's your dough."

It looked like a few thousand dollars. My fingers locked onto it but I knew I had to give it back.

"I can't accept this."

"Alright, fine."

I let go air and leaned back against the seat, relieved. Then he pushed another roll of bills onto the roll still in my hand.

"Okay, that's it. I know you're good, but that's all I'm willing to spend on that creep."

"No, no. I don't want any more money. It's just I can't shoot him. I..."

His face morphed into something demonic and he spoke in a voice of controlled rage. "Why not?"

"Well, the thing is I'm kind of specialized. I only shoot people in, uh, the entertainment industry."

"I'm afraid you'll have to make an exception this time."

Chapter Forty-Four

The policeman entered Doctor Feldman's office carrying a file folder. "As you requested, here's more evidence on Mclintock."

He quickly glanced at the many papers in the file, then nodded. "Can I keep these?"

"Why?"

"I just want to check things out a little more thoroughly."

The officer's tongue moved around the inside of his mouth as if searching for a piece of steak left from yesterday's dinner. All he found was a tiny bit of Brussels sprouts. "There's no reason to check it out. Mclintock is a scumbag. But, sure, you can keep it for a few days. Just don't show it to anyone. It's confidential."

Doctor Feldman nodded.

"Fitzgerald wanted me to give you a bonus for all the great work you've been doing for us." The officer handed the doctor a thick white envelope."

"Thanks."

The policeman opened the door and left. The doctor tore open the envelope, surprised by the huge amount of money. A moment later, worry lines appeared on his forehead as he looked around the office at the unseen "watcher."

Chapter Forty-Five

I had no clue how to get out of this. I didn't know what would come next, but I didn't say anymore to Giuseppe. I got out of the car and walked toward the photo studio. Harry Diesel's tooth-filled smile greeted me from behind the counter, having no clue that very soon, the police would be drawing a chalk outline around his body. He had on a white coat as if he were a doctor. However, the dangly jewelry hanging from his left ear, along with the fact that he was spreading hot sauce on a cheese sandwich took away from the professional medical image. Seeing me approach, he immediately moved the sandwich behind the counter. "Can I help you?"

"Is there a back way out of this place?"

"Back way?" he said, adjusting the ear jewelry with an extra long index finger. "No, I'm afraid there isn't. Why?"

I didn't answer, but then he examined me like I was an alien at Area 51 and got this frightened look in his eyes. "You're him. You're that crazy murderer I saw on TV."

"I'm not a murderer."

"Then why is that gun sticking out of your pocket?"

Great; I hadn't tucked in my gun. An amateur mistake. "Listen, Harry..."

"I changed it to Harvey. I didn't think Harry had enough pizzazz."

"Harvey, there's this guy, Giuseppe Delucca, who wants me to kill you."

"Kill me?"

"Yes."

"Why?"

"He didn't like the pictures you took at his daughter's wedding."

"That's a reason to kill a person?"

I held up the palms of my hands. "He said you made him look fat."

"He is fat."

I nodded. I couldn't argue with that.

Harvey thought a moment, then his lips turned downward. "You should kill me. He's right; I didn't do a good job on those pictures. I was sick that day, terrible flu, and I had a couple of drinks to steady my nerves. It ruined the whole thing." He held his hands up, closed his eyes. "Go ahead. I'm ready."

I blew out air. "I'm not going to shoot you."

"So why even bother coming here?"

"Well that's the thing. Giuseppe's outside, waiting for me to do it."

"Then, go ahead." He closed his eyes again.

At this point, I really wanted to shoot him, but I knew there had to be another way. A moment later, my fried brain came up with it. I would use my special talents to fake a murder. "You got anything sharp?"

He opened his eyes. "Yes, you're right. A knife is better, more agony." He pulled out a drawer and removed a small pen knife. "Go ahead, cut me." He rolled up his sleeve and held out his arm.

I ignored it. "Here's what I want you to do. Take the knife and cut yourself."

"What?"

"Get a little blood flowing. Then we spread it on my sleeve and make it look like it's blood from you getting hit with a bullet."

He had wanted to be murdered, but a little cut

seemed to make him teary-eyed. Then I thought of another approach. I opened up the jar of hot sauce on the counter, and rubbed a little on my sleeve so it looked like blood splatter. I tried to make it seem as if Harvey and I were merely talking, so Giuseppe wouldn't come in and make my actual blood splatter.

I blocked out the scene of Diesel being shot and dying. We only had one take so I had to make sure everything went off perfectly. I pretended to fire the gun and he fell to the ground. I recoiled as if the blood hit me. I believe if the Academy of Film Arts and Sciences had seen this, I would definitely have been nominated in the best acting, direction and script categories.

I told Diesel to stay on the ground for at least ten minutes. Then he should get the hell out of town. I walked out trying to look like a hit man after doing a job, which probably looked the same as normal people after they had eaten lunch.

Giuseppe's limo picked me up. "Good hit, Mclintock. I saw it through the window." He looked at the blood on my shirt. "Pretty messy, though."

I nodded. "The best kind of hit."

He leaned close to my sleeve, sniffed it. What's that smell?"

I quickly moved my arm away. "Uh, death."

"Yeah, I never get tired of that smell."

"Me neither," I said, smiling.

"But what was with all that talk?"

"Oh, he had all these excuses. He said the day he took the pictures he had too much to drink and had the flu. I told him to can it. He made you look fat."

Giuseppe pointed a finger at me. "You're ruthless. I like that."

I shrugged. "It's a ruthless game so you have to be, uh, ruthless." I wiped off the gun and handed it to

Giuseppe. Since we were getting on so well, I decided to see if he knew anything that could help me.

He thought a moment. "Onion man?"

"Yeah, he's in the game."

"Nope. Never heard of him. I did know a wise guy called 'The Tomato Man.' Took some creeps out for me. He had this real red face. Uncontrolled blood pressure. Not good for this business. He's kind of a whack job, but he knows everyone in the underground."

As he drove me back to my car, I began thinking that there were two of me. The master actor and the master criminal—like I'd played in the film *Gangland*. In that one, an actor wasn't getting anywhere so he stole money from his mother's bank account and used it to finance a criminal organization. Of course, later, when he got caught, he found out his mom had her own criminal organization. A tough film to watch, especially on Mother's Day. Giuseppe gave me the Tomato Man's address and I headed over there. First, I stopped at a Variety store and picked up some milk duds. I figured they have more nutrition than chips since they have milk in them.

The skinny clerk behind the counter had a TV and was watching some fishing show. I asked if I could change the channel for a moment. He agreed and I switched it to the news. Of course, the newscaster was Jessica Thompson.

The lead story was about a bank robbery. Luckily, my name didn't pop up for that. Then they talked about a circus coming to town. Hey, maybe the news people had forgotten about me. Suddenly, Harvey Diesel showed up on the screen. I couldn't believe it. I'd told him to leave town. He went on and on about the terrible trauma he had just been through. He said the Telemarketer-Killer had come into his shop and tried to shoot him, but Diesel had knocked him out with a right hook. Then when he turned away for a moment, the killer ran out of his shop whimpering.

Now I was a coward in addition to a murderer.

Suddenly, my least favorite person appeared.

"Dr. Feldman, I don't quite understand this. Why would Mclintock take a photographer out? He previously only dealt with people in show business—actors, agents."

The psychologist touched his beard, then spoke. "He is expanding his neurosis. At first, he sees only actors as the villains, but now he believes anyone in the arts is to blame for his lack of success."

"Is that bad?"

"In my opinion, yes, very bad. And it's only going to get worse. Soon his mind will expand the neurosis further and he will take out anyone who is successful at anything. He seems to be a very deranged individual. One of the sickest I've ever seen."

Chapter Forty-Six

Maybe I am a sicko. Normal people don't suddenly become involved with mob bosses and fake murders. That just doesn't happen to the underwear salesman at Sears. Still, no matter what, I had to find out the truth about what was going on. I left the variety store and headed over to 'The Tomato Man's' address.

He lived in a low-rise apartment in a suburban area that didn't exactly look like mob central. Some yellow roses grew in front of the drab red-bricked building giving it a bit of color. The seventy-year-old man lying on the lawn chair in front, wearing a red and green Speedo added to the festive atmosphere.

According to Giuseppe, 'The Tomato Man' lived in Apartment 402. I checked the listings at the front and found no name listed for that number. It didn't really matter. The doors were open and I could just walk right in and up to the fourth floor.

As I ambled down the hall, I could see that the door to 402 had been left open. Odd. I stepped closer, looked inside, but saw no one there. Suddenly, I felt something hard being pushed into my back. I assumed it was either a gun, or a salami way past its expiration date. A gravelly voice spoke.

"Get in."

I walked into the apartment and looked around. Only I didn't see much to look around at. The only furniture was a couch, chair and a small table with lots of medications on it.

"Sit down!"

I sat down on the ripped green leather couch that had food stains all over it. He probably had to use the gun to get people to sit on that thing.

Then I saw my kidnapper. First, the red face, then the small shrunken body and sun-wrinkled skin. He looked about eighty. The gun seemed like too much weight for him to carry as he stepped from foot to foot to balance himself.

"What's going on?" I said.

"Jenson sent you, didn't he? To take me down. I should never have trusted Francesca, especially after she killed Miguel."

"I didn't come to take you down and I don't know who any of those people are."

"Right. Then what's that gun in your pocket."

"I don't have a gun in my pocket."

He patted me down and found my keys with the cooz ball on the end.

He held it up to the light, rotated it in his hands. "The old 'cooz ball of death.' Very few are skilled enough to use it. I guess they knew they needed a master this time when all their other attempts had failed to get me. He looked at me from top to bottom, then shook his head. "But I don't think you're up to the challenge, my friend."

"I'm not a killer."

He turned the cooz ball around his hands again and stared at it as if it would attack him at any moment.

"You throw it at someone's chest at just the right angle and it causes their heart to go into spasms. Then it gradually stops beating. It's a terrible way to go. And yet beautiful." He held it up to the light. "The great thing is that no one would think it's anything other than part of a keychain." He dropped it onto the chair. "But I won't be taken down that easily. I'm as strong as an ox." He took in a deep breath, then began having a coughing fit. He grabbed a bottle of cough syrup from the table, knocking down all the other medications, and chugged it like soda. When he finished drinking it, he seemed to be out of breath. Then, he coughed again. "Yesiree, strong as an ox." He slapped the bottle down onto the table.

"Look, can you put the gun away? I'm not here to kill you."

He moved his shoulders around as if they were massaging themselves.

"You're going to break my legs?"

"No."

"Cut me?"

I shook my head.

"Encase me in cement?"

"No. I got your name from Giuseppe Delucca. He said you might be able to help me."

"I see," he said, examining my face as if he were a vet examining a schnauzer. "Alright, if you know Giuseppe, what color hair does he have?"

"He's bald."

"What does he have on his left hand?"

"A ring with a red ruby. He says he took it from a dead man."

His mouth twitched and he seemed to calm down. He lowered his gun hand and slumped into a chair, starting to breath heavy again. "This hit man stuff is tiring."

"Can I get up?"

He aimed the gun at me again. "Not yet. First I need to know what you want."

"Do you know anything about The Onion Man?"

"The Onion Man? What a ridiculous name for someone."

I stared at him a moment. "You're 'The Tomato man.'"

"It's 'TomaTOE Man,' 'TomaTOE.'" He shook his head. "I must have told Giuseppe a hundred times— 'Toe, Toe.' But he never got it. He's cool, but kind of dumb for the head of a major crime organization." He shook his head, coughed a few times, then gulped down another bottle of cough syrup.

"So you don't know The Onion man?"

"No, can't say I do. But listen kid, you need anyone hit, I'm your man. At my age, I ain't getting so many contracts to fill." He picked up his gun and began moving it around as if some enemy sniper had just appeared.

My body trembled, worried that he might actually have the strength to pull the trigger. "Sorry, I don't know anyone." I got up from the couch and grabbed my keys. "I should go."

"Okay, well, you ever need me, you know where I am."

"Yeah, thanks."

I left the "TomaTOE Man" with nothing that could help me. Nothing!

But as I walked down the stairs, something he had told me reverberated in my head.

Giuseppe had always called him 'Tomato Man,' rather than 'TomaTOE Man.' Had I gotten it wrong about the name 'Onion Man'? Had it been another name that sounded like 'onion'?

I had to go back to that restaurant and talk to the waiter.

Chapter Forty-Seven

I sat down at the same table as before. A few moments later, the curly-haired waiter came up to me.

"What would you like? Everything is good today, the fish, the cheese, the sandwiches." Then he leaned close and whispered, "Don't order the steak."

"I wanted to ask you about what you told me the other day. You know, 'The Onion Man.'"

"Oh, right."

"Are you sure that's what you heard those guys say? Cause 'Onion Man' is kind of an unusual name."

"Yeah, that's what it was. My hearing is perfect."

"Okay, good, thanks. That's all I needed to know." I stood up to go.

"Today, anyhow."

"What?"

"Today's the day I put the batteries in my hearing aid. I'm trying to conserve. Those suckers are expensive."

"So it had no batteries the other day?"

"No, but I'm a terrific lip reader. Except for certain letters. You know, like 'U,' 'N,' 'S.' Maybe 'T,' 'O,' 'L.' Sometimes 'P,' and 'A'."

"That's a lot of letters."

"They're hard to figure out. The manager is always trying to get me to use batteries every day because once in a while, I mix up a few meals. You know, like yesterday, I gave some customer a grilled cheese sandwich instead of Filet Mignon. That guy was not happy, let me tell you that. I don't know why; I was saving him from all that fatty meat."

"So, 'Onion Man' may not be the correct name."

"I'm sure it is."

"Right," I said.

"What do you want today?"

"Just some coffee." I probably pronounced the words a little louder than I should have just to be sure he understood. Of course, a few moments later, he brought me a grilled cheese sandwich.

I sat at my table substituting some of the letters he'd mentioned into 'Onion Man,' but after trying numerous variations, I gave up. I ate my grilled cheese, and left.

Chapter Forty-Eight

Doctor Feldman leaned back in his chair and began reading the reports that Harris had given him. That Mclintock was really a menace. Maybe it was right that he told the nation how he felt about him on the radio.

Yet some things bothered him. First, that meatball-breath Fitzgerald seemed a little odd. The way he acted, the way he spoke. He didn't really seem like the kind of guy who operated a medical clinic. He'd been to the website and he wasn't sure that it was even real. Then there were the three people killed by Mclintock. Two of them were patients he had sent to Fitzgerald's laboratory. That seemed very strange.

Because of his suspicions, Doctor Feldman hadn't touched the extra money that Fitzgerald had given him. However, that didn't stop him from opening up the drawer every once in a while and kissing it.

Chapter Forty-Nine

I got into my car and drove. I had no idea where I was going. I put on the radio to some country music. It tends to relax me when I hear those guys singing about losing their girl, their job, their dog. It sort of puts things in perspective. Hey, compared to them, my life was fantastic, except, of course, for the entire police force of Leaside searching for me.

The radio crackled with the DJ's voice. "And that was Lonesome Charley Rhodes, one of my personal favorites."

I switched the station so I could hear the news. I landed on a station that broadcast Jessica Thompson.

"And in other news, Jeffrey Fishman, an actor who recently got the role of Doctor Chip in a new movie—"

I stared at the radio, shocked. Fishman got that role? I hardly knew him but I'd seen his work on a couple of occasions. He was a horrible actor.

"...has just been killed. Police believe the victim was a friend of Telemarketer Joshua Mclintock."

Oh no. I yelled at the radio, "He wasn't my friend!"

"Mclintock killed Wallace Greg, Hiram Davies and almost ended the life of photographer, Harvey Diesel. Luckily, Diesel proved to be too smart for Mclintock and managed to get away. We are honored once again to have with us, Doctor Lucas Feldman, to help us understand Mclintock a little better. Doctor, why do you think Mclintock killed his friend?"

I yelled again, "We weren't friends!"

"In the acting trade, I believe there are no friends. I

have treated a number of performers but I find one common thread. They are all in competition with one another. And sometimes that can turn deadly."

"So you think Mclintock was jealous that his friend Fishman got that role. And that's why he killed him?"

I yelled again. "Listen close. He wasn't my friend!"

There was a pause. I assumed that was the doctor touching his damned beard. If he wanted to pat something, why didn't he just get a dog?

"Yes, jealousy certainly plays a part in his sick twisted mind. From my research, it seems that Mclintock had been offered that role at one point. So when Fishman got it, Mclintock exploded in a jealous rage. He is so upset by his lack of success that he is trying to get rid of everyone who is successful in any way. He is, in a sense, proving that he is a success by 'successfully' murdering people."

"Thank you, Doctor Feldman, for your always insightful thoughts."

I turned off the radio, depressed. This guy was ruining my reputation by promoting me as a sicko. The more he talked, the worse he made me look. I had to put a stop to all that, show him I was normal and that I had been railroaded.

I found his address on my phone. But I couldn't just go to see him looking like myself. He'd never let me in his office.

I opened the trunk of my car and brought out my make-up kit. I made myself up with a bald cap and glasses. I also took a plastic gun from my case that I had used in that short film about a lawyer who shot clients who didn't pay their bills on time. He didn't get a lot of repeat business.

The Feldman Clinic was located in the Standish building, off Dawson and Lawrence, a better part of Leaside.

Before I went in, I took a few deep breaths and altered my voice. I would play it a little higher but not so much that I would be mistaken for Nicole Kidman. I swiveled my jaw around, an old acting exercise, so that my dialogue would come out crisply. A few moments later, I entered the clinic and stood in front of a yellow-haired receptionist.

"Is the doctor in?"

She hardly gave me a glance. "Yes, he is. Do you have an appointment?"

I didn't have any appointment, and I couldn't wait for her to give me one. So I started walking toward the office door.

"You can't go in there!" shouted yellow hair. "The doctor is with a patient."

I ignored her like she was that acting teacher who told me I was the worst actor he'd ever seen. I'd had enough of those negative-nellies to know what to do. I walked through the doors and indeed, yellow hair was right—the doctor was seeing someone. On the couch lay a tall, good-looking man. He was talking and moving his arms around fast, as if he were a marionette whose puppeteer was on speed.

"And when I saw how enormous he was, Doc, I ran away."

"But you play a hero in all your movies."

"I'm fine on screen as the hero. But in real life," he said, blushing, "I'm a scaredy-cat."

The doctor must have heard me enter and stared at my now bald head. Feldman looked exactly the same as he had on TV. Even touched his beard a few times before speaking.

"Who are you?"

A moment later, yellow-hair marched into the office. "Doctor, I tried to stop him. He just pushed his way in."

I needed to talk to the doctor alone so I pulled out

the plastic gun and yelled, "Everyone get out!"

Yellow-hair screamed as did the man on the couch. His scream sounded more girly.

I pointed the gun at Yellow-Hair. "And don't phone the police or there'll be trouble." I wasn't lying because if she did call the police, there would be trouble—for me! Yellow-Hair ran out of the office.

The guy on the couch sat up, but seemed confused. "Is this a test, Doc?"

The doctor shook his head. "No, this is not a test."

"You want me to assert myself, don't you?"

The doctor glanced at me, then back at the large eyes of his client. "No, Mr. Simmons, now is not the time to be assertive. Just go."

The man, evidently thinking that the doctor telling him to not be assertive, was also a test, tried to give me a menacing look. Unfortunately, with his heavy breathing and his arms shaking, it made him look even more frightened. Then he said, "P-Put down the g-g-gun or I will be f-f-forced to take d-d-drastic action." He searched his pocket, finally coming out with a nail file and held it fiercely in his hand.

I smiled. "That's okay, bud, I already had a manicure." I held up my hand showing the nails Tia at "Beauty World" had lacquered three weeks ago. Then, I pointed the plastic gun at him and he dashed out like he was setting new records in running the mile.

The psychologist stood up. "What do you want?"

I took off my bald cap and glasses. The doctor's eyes opened wide and he froze. "It's you, the Telemarketer-Killer."

"Actor-Killer," I said. "It's Actor-Killer," actually feeling good that I could get that straightened out. Then I thought a moment, and realized that maybe I should not have added "killer" to the end of that sentence.

"What do you want?"

"For starters, I want you to stop saying all those bad things about me on the radio."

He put on a practiced smile, spoke calmly. "Yes, of course."

"Look, I didn't do any of those murders. I didn't kill Greg or anyone else. Everything has been some kind of frame up."

I could see the doctor's mind working, trying to figure all this out. "Of course. I know that. You didn't do any of it."

"Yes."

"Maybe you'd like to lie down on the couch and we could talk about it."

"Uh, okay. But remember, I still have the gun."

"Understood."

I lay down on the couch, my gun aimed at Doctor Feldman. He sat in the chair beside me. "So, maybe you can tell me when this started."

I gave him a little history of my career, then explained about Greg and Biggie and everything else. He didn't blink an eye, riveted on every word. I still had it! Of course, I did have the gun on him so maybe that had a little something to do with it. Maybe that's what I should do at my auditions. As I spoke, I saw his expression change from one of being baffled to one of, I don't know what. But I hoped it was good.

"I suppose it's possible. But it conflicts with all the information that I get from the police. I've been hired to, uh, analyze the case. Each week, I get information from the officer in charge. He's shared evidence with me that hasn't even been reported in the papers."

"Like what?"

"Fingerprints, DNA, eyewitnesses."

"That doesn't make any sense. I didn't do anything wrong—except run. What's the name of the officer you get your information from?"

"Harris. Jason Harris."

It felt like a cold, hard punch to my solar plexus. I'm sure my face showed surprise. I guess after a punch to the solar plexus, you would show surprise. At first, anyway, then maybe a lot of pain. "I know him. He's a bad officer."

The doctor rubbed his hands together, looked over his shoulder at the wall as if there was someone there. He seemed nervous. "Oh?"

"Look, for a while, I was hanging out with some homeless people and they said he would beat them up and plant drugs on them."

"I see."

"Will you help me?"

He looked at the wall again and stood up.

"I can't really do anything, I'm sorry. Maybe you should just go to the police."

"I can't do that." I pointed the gun at him again. "Are you sure you can't do anything?"

"I don't think a toy gun is going to make me change my mind."

The jig was up.

The doctor pointed toward the door and I walked out.

Yellow-hair looked at me like I was a murderer up on death row.

I was depressed that I was no further ahead. But a moment later, the doctor came out of his office and closed the door.

"Come with me."

Yellow hair stared at him. "Where are you taking him?"

"Oh, uh, I'm showing him where the police station is."

I didn't quite get this, but I followed the doctor as he

walked down the hall.

He didn't say anything to me and when we reached the front door, he opened it and pointed up the street. "The station's up there."

Then he looked all around, and shook my hand. "Good Luck."

I felt a piece of paper being pushed into it. I continued on my way out of the building. Once there, I looked at the piece of paper. It had an address on it and the name, Stan.

Chapter Fifty

The address turned out to be a police administration building. Why would the doctor send me here? Then it hit me. They have records in that building. He must have wanted me to check out Harris. But how would I do that? They weren't going to just give me information. I'm an actor not a policeman. Then I looked in the backseat of my car and it came to me. I put the policeman clothes back on, then drove over to the administration building.

I spoke to the gum chewing-lady at the front desk. "Where's records?"

She chewed her gum a couple of times, making a cracking sound, then spoke. "Down the hall and to the left."

I thanked her and headed down the hall. I saw the black sign up ahead with white letters that said, "Records." I entered and waited at the counter until a petite lady with big hair came over. "Can I help you?"

"Actually, I'm looking for Stan."

She nodded and a few moments later, a tall man, thin as a coat hanger greeted me. His right shoulder twitched.

"I'm investigating an officer and I need to see his record report."

He gave me a bored expression, then held out his hand. "Paperwork."

"Damn, I forgot."

"Sorry. Unless you have paperwork, I can't do anything." His left shoulder twitched.

"Actually, uh, Doc Feldman sent me, Stan. We're working together—investigating an officer. He said you might be able to help."

His lips widened into a big smile. "Oh, the doc sent you. Isn't he wonderful?" He really helped cure all my ticks." Both shoulders twitched. "Well, if the doc says it's okay, it's hunky dory with me. Whose records did you want to see?"

"Jason Harris."

The man's face turned white. "Harris?"

"Yeah. Something wrong?"

"It's just a surprise that's all. He's gotten so many awards for arrests and drug busts, it's hard to believe he's under investigation."

"It's just routine. I'm sure there's nothing there." I laughed as I figured a policeman might. Stiff.

Stan said he'd be right back.

A moment later, he returned with a thick file. I took it and was about to head out when Stan called me back to the counter.

"You can't leave the room with that."

"Oh right."

I took a quick glance through the file, saw only awards Harris had won and praise for his work. Nothing else. No mention of any disciplinarian action. There'd be no reason to keep the file. It didn't help at all.

"That's good enough." I handed it back to Stan and left.

I was hungry and depressed so I drove over to a small sandwich shop and ordered a Tuna Melt. I sat down, first wiping away the crumbs on the table and then trying to sort through what I knew. There was a police officer who got lots of drug busts by planting drugs on homeless people. So, he wasn't quite as clean or perfect as everyone thought. He had also been assigned to my case and apparently was giving fake information to Feldman. He was also dating my ex. For some reason that bothered me the most. I felt that stomach thing whenever I thought about it.

It was a lot of information, but it didn't really amount to much. I had to find something else.

Chapter Fifty-One

Jazmin called to see how things were going. I needed someone to bounce ideas off so I asked if she'd come to the restaurant. Twenty minutes later, she walked in the door looking radiant, dressed in a red blouse and short tartan skirt.

She stared at my police officer outfit, confused for a moment, then a smile peaked through. "Wow, you look good. Is that for a role?"

"No, I needed the outfit to get into the police records office."

I told her about what had happened of late.

"Wow, you've been through a lot."

I nodded. She was right; I had been through a lot. But it was effort without results. Just like my career.

Jazmin started talking, and while I loved listening to her voice usually, today, I couldn't get what she was saying. All I heard was this chopping sound from behind the counter. I looked over and saw a woman slicing tomatoes for a sandwich. She was really good at slicing. If I'd been doing that, she would have ended up with three slices of tomato and two fingers. It also reminded me of 'The TomaTOE Man.'

"Joshua, you there?"

I turned my attention back to Jazmin. "Sorry, I was thinking about something."

"What?"

"Well, there's this guy. He calls himself 'The TomaTOE Man,' but the gangster who told me his name called him 'The Tomato Man.'"

"Gangster?"

"Yeah."

She touched my hand. "You really have been through a lot."

Maybe the guy I'm looking for is not 'The Onion Man.' Maybe it's a name that just sounds like 'Onion Man.'"

"Sure, that's possible."

"I'm going to try an exercise that I used to do in improv class to help me think faster. I'm going to say a lot of words that sound like 'onion' and see if that gets me anywhere. I took a deep breath. "Onion, tunion, lunion, binion, union, hunyion smuglin, inlin..." I took another breath, then said, "Kinlin, pin..."

"Hold it. The only real word you said was 'union'."

"'Union'? 'Union.' Maybe that's it. Maybe he's the 'union' man."

"Which union? There's tons of them."

I looked down at the gold buttons on my sleeve. "Maybe it's the police union. That would make sense. It also might explain why I keep running into Harris." My mind reeled. "Maybe this thing goes all the way to the top of the police force."

Chapter Fifty-Two

I heard some sirens and my hand started to shake. I looked out the window but they'd already passed by.

"Where are you staying now?"

"Chez Toyota."

"Your car?"

"Yeah."

She put her arm on my back. "Why don't you come over to my place?"

"But the police were there before."

"That's why it's a good idea. They've already been there, so they're not going to check again."

She had a point and I decided to take her up on her offer.

We went to her place and that's when I realized how tired I was. I immediately lay down on her living room couch while she went to make some tea. I was afraid to turn on the TV to hear what they were going to say about me. But I did anyway. Of course, Jessica Thompson, my favorite newscaster was on.

"We haven't heard much from the Telemarketer Killer lately and all of us are wondering when he is going to strike again. Doctor Lucas Feldman is here with us and maybe he can shed some more light on this sicko."

Oh great, I couldn't wait. Now I was going to be forever known as "Joshua Mclintock/Telemarketer Killer/Sicko."

The doctor did not touch his beard. That was the first of many shocking things that happened.

"Jessica, I have been reconsidering this man's case."

The newscaster looked puzzled. "Reconsidering? So he's even more of a crazy than you previously thought?"

The doctor seemed to choose his words carefully. "Not exactly. I've been studying his actions a little more closely and I now believe there is a possibility that he may have been framed."

My heart sped up. This was great!

"Framed? Then who is doing the killing?"

"At this point, I can't tell you, but there may be one person or many. And they may well be members involved in some organization that we would hardly expect. But, as I say, this is just a preliminary thought."

It was preliminary, but he was actually saying I didn't do it. That definitely made me feel better.

Jazmin brought in the tea and sat down on a chair beside me. I told her what I'd just seen. She seemed surprised.

"Why the sudden turnaround?"

I picked up my tea, sipped a little. "Well, I did talk to him the other day and maybe he believed some of what I said."

"Good. So any ideas what to do next?"

"Well, if the head of the police union is involved, then I'd have to find out more. I already went to 'records' to get material on Harris but it didn't help much."

"Maybe if we went into the union office during the night and searched, we might find something."

"I doubt we'd find..."

She rubbed my shoulder. "Isn't it worth a shot? After all, you don't have any other leads right now."

"How would we get in?"

"One of my acting thingies was being a magician's assistant. I learned how to get into places that were locked. It came in handy when I wanted to check up on my boyfriends."

"I don't know. I'm already in so much trouble."

"It'll be fine."

We found out the union office was located on Chauncy Avenue and went there at two in the morning. Jazmin was right, she did know her stuff. She opened up the front door, quick as a flash, and cut the alarm so it wouldn't ring. There were several rooms down the hall, but at the end there was the president's office, J.K. Forton.

Jazmin worked the lock with a small metal pin and opened the door. We entered and I turned on the lights. In the middle of the room sat a big desk with a stack of papers piled high. Beside the papers was a picture of, I assumed, J.K. Forton and his wife sitting on the sand at the beach in their bathing suits. Both of them looked like body builders.

In the corner sat a bookcase filled with books on police work—forensics, investigation techniques. It was just like my library was filled with books on acting. Except these looked like new and mine had been so dog-eared the dog wouldn't touch them. I looked at the appointment book on the desk to see if there was anything that would help me. But all I saw were meeting times, not details. Then I saw a name I knew––Jason Harris. Forton had a meeting planned with him for today. And beside it the word 'dismissal.' I showed it to Jazmin.

"He was going to be fired?"

"I guess. Maybe they found out about some of the stuff he's been doing."

I went around to the side of the desk and wished I hadn't. There was a body on the floor, with a bullet hole through his chest. The body belonged to J.K. Forton. Jazmin cringed.

I didn't. I'm guessing because I've been around lots of so-called dead bodies in my work as an actor and according to the media, I had been the cause of some dead bodies myself.

"Do you think Forton was killed by Harris because he found out about the firing?"

I shrugged. "Hard to know."

Suddenly, I heard another voice. "Not really hard to know. I can tell you."

I looked toward the voice and saw Harris with a gun in his hand.

Chapter Fifty-Three

Dr. Feldman sat on the bench outside Markdale Park waiting for Fitzgerald. He had been anxious the last few days and couldn't see patients. They wanted their doctor to be in control, not someone with shaky hands wearing a jacket full of sweat stains.

A few moments later, Fitzgerald dressed in a pin-striped suit plopped down beside him. He took a sip of his latté, then turned toward the doctor. "You said there was something important?"

Dr. Feldman moistened his lips, then spoke quietly. "Something seems odd about our arrangement."

"Odd how?"

"I've sent you two patients and both turned up dead."

Fitzgerald shrugged. "Coincidence. You know how many people turn up dead every day?"

The doctor shook his head.

"Uh, lots. Lots and lots."

"It just seems odd that of all the actors that Mclintock could have killed, the ones he did, came from my clinic."

Fitzgerald sipped his latté.

"And something's odd in my office too."

"How so?"

"It seems as if I'm being watched."

"Watched? You're just paranoid. Everything is fine."

"Alright, but I'm going be very careful from now on in. No more patients until I feel everything is okay."

"Sure, sure." Fitzgerald finished his latté and threw the cup into the trash can. "If that's all, I gotta go." He got up and walked down the sidewalk. After a few moments, he took out his cell phone. "Carlos, we have a problem."

Chapter Fifty-Four

Harris stood in front of me smiling. "Yes, Forton found out some things. He threatened to dismiss me. There was no way I could allow that. I had a thriving drug business going on. Plus the other thing with Greg."

"What thing with Greg?"

"Not important."

"It's important to me."

"Well, it won't be in a while when 'The Group' finds you."

"What group?"

"Not important."

"Can you be any clearer about any of this stuff?"

"Afraid not. But there is one thing you should know." He smiled at Jazmin. She smiled back and sprang over to him, as if the two of them were magnets of opposite polarities. She threw her arms around his shoulders. Jazmin spoke. "We're working together."

I shook my head in disbelief.

"She was keeping track of you for 'The Group'."

My heart sank. All along I had thought she was on my side. I asked again, "What is this damned group?"

Jazmin said it, this time. "Not important."

Harris moved a little closer to me. "I will let you in on something. I'm going to shoot you, then put the gun that killed Forton in your hand. To the police, it's going to look like you took him out and then he shot you as his last act."

My mind immediately went to the theatrical. "That's

gonna be hard to stage. You'd have to be a pretty good chorographer to make that work. And judging by your two step, I don't think you have it in you."

A scowl appeared on his face. "Shut up and stand over there." He pointed to a spot near the desk.

I shook my head. "I don't think that's the right place. I should be further upstage because if I'm too close I could just hit him with the gun. But if I'm farther away it makes more sense that I fire it. You know everything is in the details."

He shook his head and let go a big sigh. "Crazy actor. Alright. Do whatever the hell you want. Just shut up."

I moved around the room, looking like I was trying to figure it out. I moved toward the body, then away from it. But each time, I would try and land a little closer to Harris, just not enough so that he would notice. Then, when I moved closest to him, I brought my hands up and punched him in the gut. Right hand, then left, then right again. Jazmin grabbed my shoulders, trying to pull me away, but I wouldn't budge.

Harris threw one back at my stomach. I was in pain, but I grabbed his gun and tried to wrestle it away from him. His fingers were curled around it like it was gold. I punched him hard. This time I got the gun free. I thought everything was fine. But then he pulled out another gun. What's with that? Who has two guns? Movies were supposed to teach you everything about life. Never saw a crook with two guns in one damn film.

"Drop it," he said.

I wanted to drop it. I really did. But I couldn't. The man was going to shoot me. I was a pacifist at heart, marched in the rally for more gun control in Leaside, although mostly because one of my co-stars from *Nude*

Bikini Models protested naked. But you know when someone has a gun pointed at your chest, it kind of changes your perspective.

I had no choice. I pulled the trigger. Got him right in the middle of his chest. He slammed onto the ground. Blood spurted out like a volcano erupting.

Jazmin started screaming, then knelt down beside him. I threw the gun down and ran out of the office like the devil was chasing me.

I kept running at top speed and didn't stop till I got to my car. I drove, not having a clue where I was headed, my brain racing with all kinds of terrible thoughts.

I had to get out of the car. I parked and ran into a field, ending up at Whitcomb Bridge. The bridge covered the murky waters of Lake Winising. The rumors were that the mob had dumped a lot of dead bodies there. But right now, there was no one around.

I was shaking, breathing heavy. I felt raw. I had just shot someone. What was I thinking? I was an actor, not some ruffian. I had done the most terrible act one human being could do to another. Yes, he was a bad guy, but still I felt the guilt to my core.

And worse yet, the one person I had trusted to help had turned on me. Or did I turn her away from me, like I'd turned everyone else away?

I was lost.

I looked at the water below. I thought of a scene I had done in the film *The Big Swim*. It was all about a swimmer who was a fanatic about what he did. He spent all of his time and energy on swimming, not devoting the time he should to the relationships in his life. When his girlfriend didn't show up at the big competition, he realized what he'd done, but it was too late. He'd lost everyone. He decided there was nothing left for him. He went to a bridge like this one. He was about to throw himself off when his girlfriend showed up. He told her that he was sorry for not spending more time with her. She forgave him, then the two of them drove to the competition. He won. That was the movies for you. Always a happy ending. In real life, at least in mine, not so much. Nobody would come at the last minute to say they loved me. I was alone as I always had been and always would be. It was fitting I was at a bridge, because I had burned so many of them in my life.

I sat down and dangled my feet over the edge, looked down at the dark water, the waves rolling in and out. I was seeing my life more clearly than ever before. My acting career had been a total farce. At the same time, I had wrecked everyone else's life too. And now so many people hated me. The mob, the police, Jazmin. Even Randy. My life was over.

And maybe it should be.

I pulled myself up to the railing and looked down. The water below beckoned me to join it. Like a carnie at some fair calling a sucker over to try and hit the balloons with darts and win the big purple stuffed dog. My body shook, but I knew jumping was the only way out. At least I'd have peace. I steadied myself on the railing, ready to say goodbye to the world. I closed my eyes.

I lifted my foot.

Suddenly, I felt something. Was I imagining it or was it real? Was it my guardian angel? I turned to my right and saw a hand on my shoulder. It was warm and strong and comforting.

Maybe there was someone who cared. Maybe I hadn't alienated everyone. Maybe there was still a single person in the world who thought I was worthwhile. By the strength of the arm holding me, I could tell it was a man. A kind man, a good man. He pulled me to my feet and off the bridge. That's when I felt how powerful he was.

He put his arm around me and moved me forward toward his car.

Chapter Fifty-Five

Fitzgerald chugged down his third drink at Brandy's Bar and Grill. Then he tapped his glass on the table.

Sam the bartender grimaced. "You really think you should have another? You've already fallen off your bar stool twice."

"Testing my agility. Now pour."

Sam shrugged. "Okay." He filled Fitzgerald's glass. "What's so bad anyway that you have to drown your sorrows?"

"Business things. Everything was going well and then this moron got involved and screwed it all to hell."

"Yeah, I have a brother-in-law like that too."

Fitzgerald shook his head, knowing the idiot bartender didn't understand the depth of the situation.

He chugged his drink down and immediately felt better, more mellow.

A moment later, Carlos, white as a sheet, ran into the bar. "Something bad happened."

"What?"

"Harris. He's dead."

Fitzgerald stared at Carlos for a moment, then fell off his bar stool.

Chapter Fifty-Six

The man leaned me against his car. "Lucky I got you before you jumped off that bridge."

I nodded, not expecting this man to be my savior. But maybe love was in everyone's heart.

"I don't want nothing to happen to you."

"Thanks."

"Before I kill you." Giuseppe smiled.

Maybe not so much love.

He looked me over. "Why you doing yourself in? Not enough hits?"

"Yeah, something like that."

"You know this might interest you, Mclintock. I was driving down the street the other day and saw something I never thought I'd see. Customers were coming out of Diesel's photography studio. Do you know why that would be?"

I shrugged.

"I thought at first, maybe his son took over the business of his dear departed father, but no, that wasn't it. Diesel is alive and doing photography. Pretty weird huh?"

"I, uh, guess the bullet missed him. You know, maybe the sites were off on that gun you gave me, and the bullet hit the wall instead of him."

"Certainly possible. But I know satisfying customers is important to you. That's why I'm giving you another chance. This time, I'm going to make sure you follow through. Got it?"

I didn't say anything. In my fragile state, I didn't

care anymore what happened to me. He pushed me into his car and we drove to Diesel's studio. Giuseppe pulled me out of the vehicle and gave me another gun. He said not to worry about how many bullets I used. Very generous of him.

I walked into the studio. Diesel stood behind the counter with a big grin which slowly faded when he saw me.

I moved close to him. "What are you still doing here? I told you to get out of the country."

"The thing is I had a couple of wedding things to finish."

"Yeah, well I got some bad news for your customers; they may not be getting their prints."

"Why not? I finish everything I start."

I rolled my eyes. "Because Giuseppe told me to kill you again." Harvey started to shake as he stared at something in back of me like a vampire noticing the sun coming up.

Then I realized what Diesel was staring at. Giuseppe had come into the shop and was walking over to the counter.

"Hello, Harvey, nice to see you're alive and well."

Diesel smiled. "Thank you. You're looking like you, uh, lost a few pounds. Atkins must really be working for you."

Giuseppe pulled a gun out, about to shoot probably both Diesel and me when, suddenly, the door swung open and a white-haired lady who looked like she was in her eighties marched in.

She came over to the counter and smiled at a frozen Diesel. "Are my pictures ready yet?"

Harvey didn't move.

"Can I get them this year?"

Harvey looked at Giuseppe who nodded.

"Yes, Miss Sanders. They're in the back." He left to

get them.

She saw the gun in Giuseppe's hand so I thought I'd better calm her down. I turned to Giuseppe. "Yes, sir, you do look like Al Capone in that get up."

He looked at me puzzled.

"It's going to make a delightful Christmas card."

The lady responded, almost growling. "The man looks nothing like Al Capone." She smiled. "I dated Capone."

I shook my head to the lady. "No, no, he does. You know in the right light and with..."

"I don't think so."

Giuseppe gave her an intense stare like the one I'm sure he gave to all his future victims.

She gave the same look right back to him. "You don't have the toughness. Look, I can take that gun right out of your hand." And amazingly enough, she did just that. "See, you're too soft."

Giuseppe looked stunned. "Lady, give me that..."

She turned the gun around in her hands. "You need a real weapon too. This one looks so much like a fake it's unbelievable. You couldn't even knock out a copper with it. See..." She bopped Giuseppe on the head and he fell to the ground.

She looked at him and started laughing. "That's funny, like anyone would get knocked out with this gun. Does it even fire? She pointed it at us."

I nodded, terrified. "Yes, yes, it does. Be careful." A shot rang out and the sign advertising passport photos for twenty dollars banged onto the ground.

I grabbed the gun from her and put it on the counter. "He doesn't like people touching his weapons."

She looked down at Giuseppe's unconscious body. "I can't believe he's still pretending to be knocked out."

"Yeah, he's quite a kidder," I said.

A moment later, Harvey came back with the lady's

pictures. She paid and left the studio.

Then it was just the three of us, leaning on the counter. Three? What? I looked over and saw Giuseppe beside me holding the gun on us. He had gotten up quicker than I thought he would.

"Okay, guys, this is it. You're gone-ers." He had us stand in front of the counter while he moved a little ways back so as not to make everything too bloody when he fired the gun. I believe that's one of the principles of Feng Shui.

I knew I had to do something, but all that came to my mind was one phrase. You'd think it would be something like "The good die young," or "Think happy thoughts." No, it was something Titus Levinsky had said: "Remember the goat."

And I did. I kicked the gun right out of Giuseppe's hand, then, taking advantage of the surprise, kicked him in the middle of his forehead. He fell to the ground, unconscious. Again.

Don't tell me acting can't save lives.

Harvey thanked me, then shook my hand. I told him to phone the police. He decided that maybe this time, he would leave town and perhaps open up a photography studio in Ecuador.

I left Giuseppe where he was, figuring the cops would take care of him. But I got out of there as quickly as I could just the same.

It felt great saving Harvey's life. Maybe I was a worthwhile person. Maybe there was something good in me after all.

I left the studio, walked over to the limo and spoke to the driver. I told him that Giuseppe had said to wait. "He was figuring out the right angle to shoot the creep to give him the most pain." The driver nodded and smiled.

I headed down the street, passing lots of ferns that

the city had planted on the sidewalks and inhaled their beautiful aromas. My spirits were high, even though I was still a wanted man. But maybe I had turned things around somehow, you know, with that law of attraction thing. You attract good luck when you do good things.

I got back into my car and started driving. After a few moments, I looked out the window and saw the first good omen. It was the Leaside Repertory Theatre.

Something had drawn me here.

I stopped the car and dashed across the road, feeling ecstasy inside. I opened the heavy wooden doors and walked into the lobby of the theatre. I looked at the red carpeted floor and the velvet-like wall-paper and was immediately bombarded by the spirits of all the greats who had been members of the troupe. It felt as though they were welcoming me with open arms. There was no one in the lobby, but I heard actors performing.

I opened the theatre doors and entered. On stage, I saw a few men and women wearing medieval costumes, rehearsing.

I recognized one of them—Sir Roger Simmons. He wore a beard and crown, sat in a golden throne. He was an Englishman who had been knighted by the queen for his starring role in *Pirandello*. He looked at me and frowned, then spoke in that resonant voice of his. "Sir, what are you doing here? There are no performances today."

"I wanted to have an audition."

"We are not auditioning now. Please leave."

I wouldn't let that deter me. Some amazing life force had brought me here. It couldn't have been for just another rejection.

"No."

"No?"

"You guys don't know what I've been through, how many times I've been close to death in the last week.

I've been chased by police, ordered to do a hit by a mobster, almost killed by a theatrical agent, backstabbed by a girl who turned out to be working for a crooked cop and shot a man. I don't know how much time I have left. If I was a cat, I would have lived eight of my nine lives."

The man stared at me a moment. "I'm sorry, nothing I can do."

"There must be someth..."

"We are not auditioning. Leave."

I rubbed my eyes, my world falling apart. I headed toward the door.

"Wait."

I froze for a moment, then swung around. One of the women on stage had spoken. "I know you. You played Gertrude in that production of *Hamlet* at the 'Summer in the Park Festival' last year."

"Yes, we were trying to create the way it would have been done in Shakespeare's time, you know with men playing the women's parts. Also, we couldn't find any actresses who wanted to work with us."

She stared at me, thinking something over. "Give us a moment."

She and the others whispered to one another, then she turned back to me. "Alright, come here at midnight."

"Midnight?"

"Yes. We will audition you tonight at midnight. But if you don't show up or are late by one minute, the audition is cancelled. Got it?"

I couldn't breathe for a moment, then I said. "Yes, midnight, I'll be here. Thank you so much."

I left, my heart racing like I was a six year old who had just seen Santa for the first time. I was finally going to have the audition I'd waited for my whole life. I felt like doing a jig except that last time I'd done that, I'd made a hole in my apartment floor and fell into the laundry room in the basement. So I decided against it.

It was only eight o'clock now, so I had a couple of hours to kill. I couldn't decide what to do, but then I saw a newspaper ad for 'The Leaside Film Festival.' At least this way I could hide out in a theatre and watch some cool movies.

The festival, as always, was held at the Eldridge Theatre, one of the oldest movie theatres in Leaside. The great thing was that the police generally stayed away from that area of town, knowing they could get themselves into trouble. If they arrested a Jack Nicolson or a Colin Farrell for jay walking or having a spat with an autograph seeker, I'm sure the Mayor would come down hard on the police department.

There was always a party before the films started and sometimes celebrities appeared.

I entered the Eldridge, and paid. It cost some big Deniros so that you could hopefully see a Deniro or a Kingsley or a Cruise. Usually, I didn't have the cash to go. But tonight, thanks to my benefactor, Giuseppe, I could see all the films I wanted and hang out at the parties.

I noticed a lot of people milling around. Originally, these parties were meant just so the stars could hang out together. However, the Festival people decided to make this a money-making venture and began selling tickets to the public. But then fewer and fewer actual stars showed up because they didn't want to be bothered with people asking them for their autographs every minute. So now they had what was advertised as a star-filled get-together, dominated by the lighting guy, the camera person and the gaffer. But there were still a few stars who came such as Kate Capshaw, and Eric Roberts.

In the corner of the ballroom I saw Laura Wilcox

from A-1 Talent, a small agency. She had wanted me as a client years earlier. I had always thought she was beneath me, but now that Biggie had let me go, I felt differently.

I'd forgotten how attractive Laura was. Blonde hair, long sexy legs and a two-hundred-watt smile. "Hey, Laura!"

"Joshua." She kissed me on my cheek. One of my favorite erogenous zones. Actually, anywhere on my body or within a two mile radius of my body is a favorite.

"How are you doing?"

"Good," I lied.

"Didn't I read something about you in the paper?"

Before she got too far on that track, I decided to change the subject. "Listen, I wondered if you would consider taking me on?"

"Taking you on?" She recoiled like a turtle sticking his neck back into it's shell.

"What about Biggie?"

"He let me go."

"Oh, I'm sorry. What happened? That was a long relationship."

I shrugged. "Just one of those things."

She stared at me a moment. "You want me to represent you."

I nodded.

"Well, correct me if I'm wrong, here, Joshua, but didn't I ask you to join us about five years ago? Before Biggie? I believe your comment was, 'Laura, I'm on my way up. Your agency isn't big enough for me.'"

"You know I don't remember. I was drinking a lot in those days."

"Look, I was full of myself back then. I've been through some stuff since and I think I've learned a thing or two. You know I'm good. You've seen the stuff I've done. Wouldn't it be worth it to add me to your roster?"

She looked down at her red pumps. Maybe the color made her think better. When she lifted her head back up, she had a smile on her face. "Okay, fine. But you're on probation. We'll give it a month or two and see how it goes. Come to my office on Monday and we'll discuss things."

"Thanks a lot, Laura." I kissed her, careful not to give her the Mclintock-lip lock.

She said she saw someone she needed to talk to and left.

It didn't bother me. It was the Hollywood way. You see someone more important and you leave whomever you're talking with.

It was turning out to be great day. I now had an agent and at midnight there was that audition with the Leaside Repertory Company. Plus, I was at the Film Festival just hanging out. How much better could life get?

Leaning against the bar in the corner was Manuel Selman, a Spanish director I had worked with before. He had long black hair and a strange triangular face that Isosceles would have spent hours trying to figure out. I walked over.

He smiled, showing perfect white teeth. "Hello, my friend. How are you enjoying the party?"

I shared with him my extensive knowledge of the Mexican language, "Mucho."

"That's great. Your Spanish is really improving, Joshua." He laughed.

"I was curious," I said. "Did you see Tom Findley's new movie?"

"Yes, fantastic."

"Didn't you think something was lacking from Findley's performance. It seemed as if he was just going through the motions."

He nodded as I spoke, then looked away, spotting someone. "Excuse me; I have to go."

The Hollywood Way.

He walked over to Walter Bingham, one of the hot new actors. I'd seen him many times before. But now he looked different somehow. The same way the other people I'd had contact with, had looked different. I still didn't know what all that meant.

At eight, the bell rang indicating the movie was about to start. It was called *A Ruined Life* and it wasn't my first choice as the title reminded me too much of my own life.

It opened on a couple who were enjoying themselves at a carnival when the man got shot in the arm. The movie was okay but as I watched Bob Timara, playing the lead, I was shocked. I'd seen him many times before, but the passion, the ability to make the audience feel, the emotion was gone. And again...he didn't look like his usual handsome self.

Something was wrong with all the actors I'd seen.

Chapter Fifty-Seven

Doctor Feldman left the betting window and hurried to his seat. His psychic had told him he would be a big winner today. Of course, she had been wrong about him not getting indigestion from that chili. But he had hopes.

He grabbed a hot dog and sat in the front row of the track waiting for the race to begin. A moment later, however, he felt an arm around his shoulder. He turned to look at a dark-skinned man in a T-shirt. He had a permanent sneer on his face and muscles the size of basketballs.

"Hey Doc."

"Do I know you?"

"We haven't been formally introduced, but I am very familiar with you."

"What do you want?"

"We're going on a little trip."

"I just placed a bet."

The man lifted the doctor out of his seat and began dragging him to his car.

"But the psychic told me I was going to..."

The man didn't say anything, just squeezed him into the back seat of his Ford Fiesta.

"Where are you taking me?"

"You'll find out soon enough. But, first..." The man wrapped a blindfold around the doctor's eyes.

"Did Tony send you? I have the money to pay him. Didn't that hug mean anything to him?"

Chapter Fifty-Eight

I had to talk to someone about the actors. But who? Then it hit me—Kennedy. He was, after all, the head of SAG, the main acting organization in Leaside.

It was about ten o'clock in the evening and I figured he wouldn't be at the office till morning. Luckily, I knew where he lived. I had been there once or twice or thirteen times before to protest something or other. But today I was here for something much more important. I had to make him understand that something bad was going down.

Shirley, his trophy wife answered the door. She still looked beautiful even at the ripe old age of twenty-seven. She wore short shorts that really showed off her long, athletic legs. She had a perfect smile that slowly dissolved when she saw it was me. She was an actress at one time and she was probably jealous that I was still in the business and she wasn't anymore. "Hey, Shirl, I need to see Kennedy."

"He's gone to sleep."

I could tell she wasn't going to let me in. Sometimes you just have an instinct about these things—her knuckle-white fingers on the door, and the fact that she was now closing it in my face. I didn't have time to waste. I squeezed through the door before she closed it. She shouted, "Joshua, hold it."

I didn't stop. I couldn't stop. I was a man on a mission. I saw Kennedy in the living room sitting on the couch. Two men sat on other chairs.

I spoke quickly, knowing I didn't have much time to

get my message out. "Kennedy, I have to talk to you. It has huge ramifications for the entire industry."

Kennedy rolled his eyes and sighed.

The man with glasses looked at me a moment. "Isn't he that criminal in all the papers, Austin?"

"Yeah," said the other man, rubbing his moustache. "He's the guy the cops are looking for."

Glasses nodded. He took out his cell phone. "Should I call the police, Kennedy?"

Kennedy shook his head. "No, I'll talk to him." He got up from his chair and told his friends to go. Then he closed the door and had Shirley leave the room.

I sat down on the plastic covered couch, my butt sticking to it like butter to bread.

Kennedy growled. "What in hell's name is so important, Mclintock? You got screwed again by another prodco?"

"No, it's not that, see..."

"Why don't I give you a dollar and you can keep it in escrow the next time you feel short changed."

"I leaned in close, whispered, "Something is happening to the actors in this town."

"You mean, unlike you, they're actually getting work?"

It was a low blow, but I ignored it. "Have you seen any movies lately?"

"Sure, lots of them.'"

"Haven't you noticed how the actors don't look the same? Not only that, but their performances are substandard. The heart is missing, the passion, the soul. Something is going on and it's wrong. I know it in my gut."

He blew out air, making his lips flop around. "I think I know what's going on."

"You do?"

"Yeah."

"What?"

"Jealousy."

"Jealousy?"

"Mclintock, you've been at this a while and haven't made it. So you have to make up all these wild accusations to get attention, since you're not gonna get it from your work."

I stood up, furious. "No, that's not it at all. Maybe I haven't been the most successful actor in town, but every performer worth his salt puts everything he has into all his performances, small or large. If this was just about one or two actors, I'd say, well, maybe he's getting old, or he had a bad surgery job or the script wasn't as good as it should be. But it's everyone and we owe it to the industry to get to the bottom of this."

He examined me like I was a specimen under a microscope, then spoke softly. "Look, Mclintock, I've got things to do. Go."

I could see I wouldn't get anywhere with Kennedy. I left, worried that it was already too late.

Chapter Fifty-Nine

If Kennedy wouldn't listen, what could I do? Besides, it was eleven thirty-three. I had to get to The Leaside Repertory Theatre. It would only take about ten minutes from where I was, so I didn't have to rush. But I thought I'd give myself some extra time by leaving now. I got in my car and began driving.

My cell rang.

"Hello?"

"Joshua, it's Randy. I need to talk to you."

Randy? I hadn't talked to her since she'd thrown me out. She told me she didn't want to see me anymore. And yet she was calling.

"What's wrong, Randy?"

"I can't tell you on the phone. Can you come over?"

"Now?" I couldn't do now. My career hung in the balance.

"Randy, I can't. I have this thing. How about tomorrow morning?"

"It's too late."

"But that's the..."

She clicked off.

I felt bad. But what could I do? I'd waited my whole life for this audition. It was my one and only chance. I'd see her tomorrow.

I recited some of the lines from *King Lear* to myself, getting more excited by the moment.

I parked in front of the theatre and raced to the front door. I spent a moment looking at the marquee. They had pictures of my favorite actors—Jeff Harris, Cynthia

Coleman, Charlie Rhodes. Then, under coming attractions, they listed *King Lear*. I visualized myself playing to a packed house dressed up as...the funny thing is, usually I had no trouble imagining that. But now, Randy's voice kept echoing in my head.

I realized that, once again, I'd put acting ahead of Randy. In the past when she'd truly needed me I hadn't been there for her. I wanted to be, but there was always an audition, a read through of a script, a meeting with Biggie. I had given up alcohol, but I was still addicted to my other drug—acting.

I called the theatre and told them I couldn't make it tonight and asked if I could reschedule the audition. They said I couldn't.

I sat for a moment in the car, grieving for my lost opportunity. Then I turned the car around and sped over to Randy's place, hoping I wasn't too late to help her. I didn't know what she wanted. But only now, thinking back, did I realize that her voice had sounded tense, strained.

Edith greeted me at the door, tears falling. "Randy's gone."

Chapter Sixty

Doctor Feldman sat blindfolded in a chair waiting. For what, he had no idea. He only knew he was out five hundred bucks from the bet at the track.

The door creaked open and he heard a familiar voice. "Doctor Feldman, so nice to see you again. Well actually, I guess I can see you, but you can't see me." The man laughed.

"Fitzgerald?"

"Yes. How are you doing, Doc? Everything okay?"

"I'm blindfolded. I'm out five hundred dollars. I'm not okay."

"I'm concerned about you. There must be something terribly wrong. Perhaps a mental imbalance. We were paying you good money and yet you got it into your head to say that Mclintock might not be guilty."

"I had to say what I thought. Something is going on. And I think you're behind it all."

"That's not the way to talk to the man who's been helping you clear up your gambling debts. You don't want Tony coming back and doing something to your scrotum do you?"

A thought suddenly hit Doctor Feldman. "You. You're the one who's been bugging my office."

"That's right. And it was a good idea. The way you're acting, you might just say something stupid to the wrong person."

"Doesn't matter. I want you to go back on TV and tell everyone you made a mistake. Mclintock is really a dangerous man and should be put in a insanity ward.

Got it?"

"And if I don't?"

Fitzgerald smiled. "Then you will be terminated."

Chapter Sixty-One

I stared at Edith's sad face. "Where is she?"

"I don't know."

"But she called me."

"When I got home a few moments ago, the place was a mess, like there had been a fight. Then I found a piece of paper that Randy had scribbled on." She handed me the paper, her eyes tearing up.

All I could make out were two words, "Joshua, danger."

"Don't worry, I'll find her, Edith." I said it as strongly as I could, knowing I wasn't all that sure, I could.

"Thank you." She hugged me; then, as if remembering something, moved away. "Look, I know I haven't been so nice to you over the years..."

I shook my head. "It doesn't matter now."

Edith paused, then looked at me for a moment. "You didn't have anything to do with this, did you?"

"No, I..."

"That's what Harris said."

I shook my head in disbelief. "Harris? You talked to Harris? When?"

"He phoned about half an hour ago, told me you were responsible for Randy being taken."

How was that possible? I had killed him. I couldn't tell Edith. She'd never be able to swallow that.

"Were you responsible, Joshua?"

I shook my head "no," not sure I wasn't somehow at fault.

I left, got in my car and drove as fast as I could. I figured that my first stop should be the police station where Harris worked. I knew he was somehow behind this. But why would he want Randy? And how was he still alive? I had seen the bullet go right into his chest.

And then it hit me on the head. He didn't want her. He wanted me. Everything pointed to that. Harris had apparently made up evidence saying I was the one who had killed all these people and he had come to the records office to shoot me. He kidnapped Randy knowing I would come to find her.

I drove to the station, not sure what I was going to do. But as I got out of the car, I saw someone reading a newspaper with Harris' picture on it. The headline read, "Jason Harris to Be Sworn in as Head of Leaside Police Department."

This was terrible.

The article said the ceremony was talking place at Langly Hall, Room C.

Five minutes later, I walked into a room filled with policemen sitting on chairs watching the current chief speaking from behind a podium. I took a seat at the back.

"On very few occasions, do we have an officer who has done so much for the community. He has made a record number of arrests and, for those of you who don't know, he recently brought down a drug kingpin. The chief pointed to a large photo on the wall behind him. It was a picture of a table full of drugs and Shorty in handcuffs.

"We are delighted to have him head up the police department as I retire from the force. Everyone, please welcome Jason Harris."

The crowd burst into applause. Harris walked up to the podium, looking no worse for being dead, except he looked different too.

I looked down the aisle of seats and was surprised to see who was in the last row—Kennedy. What did he have to do with this?

Then it came to me in a blinding flash. I had been totally wrong about everything.

Chapter Sixty-Two

The police union wasn't behind all that had happened. It was the actor's union. And the head of that was Kennedy. It explained a lot—the fact that all the actors seemed to be different now and so many people in the entertainment business were dying. I didn't know how that part would play into things yet, but I was sure it would.

Harris began talking. "Thank you very much. I look forward to taking this city in new directions." He continued with how the city was going to be much safer for everyone.

After he finished speaking, some others stood up saying how great the city was going to be under Harris. I walked out into the hall, took a drink from the tap, trying to figure out what my next move should be. It seemed to be made for me when I felt a gun in my back.

"Let's go for a nice drive, Mclintock." It was Kennedy.

As we headed outside to his car, I saw Harris behind him.

Kennedy, Harris and I drove to the Four-Ten Freeway, then took the Bernard cutoff and turned right onto Leslie Street. I'm not sure, but I believed we were the only crooks on the road, other than the guy in the Lexus throwing litter out his window.

"Where are we going?" I asked.

"Shut up."

About twenty-five minutes later, we stopped at a large green building hidden by a group of trees. It was near where I had met Shorty and the others. The building had no windows.

Kennedy hustled me inside, then down a long hallway into a small room. Livingstone and some of the goons I'd seen before were involved in an animated discussion. At the back were several tables. A man sat at one of them drinking a glass of wine and smiling at me. A sinister smile.

The first one I'd seen on Biggie.

He spoke to the other men in the room. "Guys, guys, give us a minute, will ya? I'd like to talk to my old friend in private. I think he deserves that." They all scurried out.

"Have a seat, Joshua."

I sat down, gave him steely eyes. "Where's Randy, Biggie?"

"Biggie yelled to someone and moments later, a man dragged Randy into the room. She was tied up, duct tape across her mouth. She looked pale, scared. And though she struggled to say something, I couldn't understand it.

"You okay?" I asked.

She nodded.

I glared at Biggie. "She has no part to play in any of this. Let her go."

Biggie waved his hand and the man took her out.

"I'm afraid I can't do that."

"She doesn't know anything, Biggie."

"I'm afraid just being aware of this place is enough to get her in trouble." He glared at me. "And unfortunately, you know too much too."

"I know that Kennedy is involved and something is happening with all the actors."

He took a sip of his wine. "You're smarter than I thought, Joshua."

"What's going on, Biggie?"

"A lot. You see lately, the industry has been having some problems. The salaries of actors are getting higher and higher and with the bad economy the studios aren't able to pay them those salaries anymore. So the problem is what do they do? Do they close up the studios and make no money, or figure out a way to keep things going at a lower budget. Now low budget movies..."

"What are you talking about, Biggie?"

He didn't seem to notice my interruption and just continued.

"...don't make any money. And some of us were worried the industry would keel over and we'd lose our jobs. On top of all this, when we've had industry meetings, everyone would complain."

"About what?"

He glared at me. "Temperamental actors." He poured more wine into his glass. "We, the agents, knew how bad they are. I mean, some of our actors..." He moved forward in his chair, emphasizing the words. "...would even call us up asking us if we thought their hair was okay the way it was or what jacket they should wear—many times a day." He was obviously talking about someone like me. Maybe actually, me. I had called him up to ask about my hair and jacket more than a few times.

So we didn't know what to do. The studios couldn't lower salaries or there would have been a huge backlash. It was a terrible situation. Kennedy or, as he likes to be called, 'John Fitzgerald,' 'cause he imagines he's like John Fitzgerald Kennedy..." Biggie rolled his eyes. "...knew there had to be a better way.

And one day in talking to talent agent Wallace Greg, he found it. Greg said how it was difficult to do all the things he had to do, make speeches, run his talent agency. Keep up the brand. So he came up with the idea of having someone impersonate him. After a lot of searching, Greg found someone who looked like him. Oh, he wasn't perfect, so Greg got make-up artists and voice people to work on him."

"That's why the pictures of Greg looked different."

"Yes, but most people never really noticed the difference and, if they did, he would explain it away by saying he'd lost a few pounds or he got a little work done. Most people were fine with that." Biggie took a swig of his wine. "When Kennedy heard about this, he knew he'd found a way so all of us could make a decent profit and not have to deal with these annoying morons anymore. We'd get rid of the real actors and switch them for people who looked and sounded like them. That way we could control things and make lots more money."

"So, that's why all the actors lacked that special something; they just looked like them. They didn't have their talent."

"'Fraid so." Biggie smirked. "We buried the real actors in different areas of Leaside so no one would be the wiser."

"Like burying Marty in that graveyard."

"Right."

"When you found his body, we knew we had to get rid of you. You caused us more problems when you shot Harris. Of course, we didn't need to replace Marty. He was only a bit player. Of no value. No one knew he even existed."

That hurt. Marty had a lot more talent in his little finger than a lot of the big actors. He just never got the chance to prove it.

"Harris was another story. We had to find a substitute for him and very quickly, because he was up for the chief's job. Thankfully, the 'new' Harris is working out just fine. And now that he's chief, we don't have to worry about any problems any more." He chugged the rest of his wine, stood up. "Why don't you come and meet some of our guys?"

Chapter Sixty-Three

Biggie and I took an elevator down to level C1. The door opened and I saw numerous cubicles, each housing a different actor—Tom Cruise, Hugh Jackman, even Eddie Murphy. Only they weren't the originals.

"This is our training room, Joshua. Here we help the imposters with their voices, their movements, and apply their make-up." He pointed to a bald man in the corner. He looked just like Bruce Willis. Even had that fiery expression Willis had near the end of *Die Hard*.

Biggie smiled. "Isn't he perfect?"

I had to admit he was. I bet Bruce's mom couldn't tell the difference.

"The replacement already looked a lot like him. He was renting himself out to L.A. parties as Bruce. But now with the makeup and some vocal work, he will actually become him."

It made me sick to my stomach. Doing all this in the name of money, sacrificing art. "Bastard."

"It's the way of the future, Joshua. These guys are so excited to be making a decent salary for a change, they don't ask for any more money. And if they do, or if there's other problems, we just get rid of them. There's a thousand more Bruce Willis look-alikes in the country."

"There may be a thousand more that resemble Bruce. But none that have his talent, his artistry."

"And at least we won't be getting anymore calls from actors in the middle of the night asking if they should give their character a stutter." He glared at me.

I shrugged. "I only did that twice, Biggie."

He smiled, "Seventeen times. But no more. You know, the sad part is that without all your tics and annoying behaviors, you're actually a great actor. You probably could have been a star if you weren't so damn irritating. We could have just gotten rid of you, but you've brought so much attention to this operation that people might wonder if you were suddenly gone. So we've decided to keep you around—just not in your present form."

"What do you mean?"

Biggie waved to someone. "Over here."

A moment later, standing beside me was—me!!! Only superficially, of course. He didn't have my magnetic ocean blue eyes, or my sensual lips.

Biggie stood. "Joshua, meet Standish O'Leary. Soon to be Joshua Mclintock."

"The man smoothed his hair back and, oh no, gave me the Mclintock double wink."

"Nice to meet you, partner."

But where was my soft, velvety voice?

Biggie tapped him on the shoulder. "Standish, we told you about the 'partner' thing. Mclintock doesn't say that."

"Oh, right, sorry. I'll go work on it."

Standish left, the Mclintock-strut nowhere to be found.

"I'd rather be dead than be part of this."

"Don't worry; that's all part of the plan."

"I'll get you, Biggie. I'll get you."

Biggie called over a short man with dark curly hair. "Carlos, take him to the room."

"What room?"

"It's where we keep all the real actors until we have the replacements' looks and voices exactly right."

Carlos pushed a gun in my back and walked me

down the hall to a door. He opened it and threw me inside.

The room had no furniture and the yellow paint on the walls was peeling. On the ground, looking dead were Tom Cruise, Eddie Murphy, Bruce Willis and others equally famous. I sniffed the air. "What's that smell?"

Carlos smiled. "It's gas that's released into the room every five minutes to keep you guys sleeping peacefully—until we need to record your voices for the replacements. Then we kill you." Carlos left and slammed the door shut.

I sat on the floor, getting sleepier by the moment. It would soon be all over. I'd be dead and replaced by an actor who didn't even know how to do the Mclintock slow-wink properly.

I stared at the actors' bodies a moment and I swear I saw someone's eye flicker. Must have been my imagination. No, there it was again. I looked closer and saw it belonged to—Deniro. Robert Deniro.

I quickly reached under Tom Cruise and pulled Deniro's body out. He was dazed at first, but gradually became conscious. Then he stared at me a moment. "You."

"Yes." I nodded, thrilled that he recognized me.

"Didn't you break into my house and I had to call security?"

"Yes, but there's no time to talk about those good times now. Can you walk?"

"I think so." He held my shoulder as he stood up. Then he began moving around the room.

"How is it that you're awake?"

"My nose was under Tom Cruise. His great abs protected me from inhaling too much of the gas."

"Great." It was, but how was I going to get out of here and find Randy before they did something to her—

if they hadn't already?

As if reading my mind, Deniro pulled a key out of his sock. "I have this. It's a universal key. Opens the inside and outside of the room. I pick-pocketed Carlos, waiting for the right moment to use it."

"Why would they need a key for the inside?"

"Apparently, Carlos isn't the brightest crayon in the box and locked himself in here a couple of times. So he had a universal key made."

At that moment, I heard the sounds of a fan. More gas was being pumped into the room. I was already beginning to feel faint.

Deniro looked sleepy too. "We gotta open the door now, the gas is instantaneous. It'll put us back to sleep in a minute."

I trudged to the door, pushed the key into the lock and turned. I started to black out, but as soon as the door opened, and I could smell clean air, my energy began to return. Deniro looked better too.

"Bob, we gotta..."

"It's Mr. Deniro."

"Right. Okay, you get everybody up and take them to the front of the building. I'll join you there. I have to go find someone."

Deniro grinned. "You looking at me?"

I smiled back, remembering the great line from *Taxi Driver*. "Yeah, yeah I am."

I rushed out and ran down the hall, desperate to find Randy.

There were a series of rooms, all locked. But using Deniro's key, I managed to open them all up. There were more actors in each who were unconscious. The last room I entered, looked empty at first, then I saw a pale Randy in the corner, her eyes shut. I wasn't sure she was still breathing. I sped over to her.

"Randy, Randy, please, come back. I love you."

She didn't move.

I shook her and, a moment later, her eyes slowly opened. "Joshua we're going to have a wonderful life together." She moved close, kissed me. She was obviously remembering our wedding. It was a great kiss, like our first. Something I had wanted to feel again for a long long time. I wanted to leave my mouth on hers forever. But time was of the essence. I slid my lips off hers.

"Randy, are you okay?"

"I do." Her eyes blinked, and reality seemed to pop into her brain. She looked at me. "Where are we?"

"It's a long story."

"Did I just say, 'I love you'?"

I took a deep breath. "No, of course not. Why would you say something stupid like that?"

"It just seemed that I..."

"We have to get out of here."

We left the room and marched down the hallway to the front of the building. I saw Deniro there, waiting with a whole raft of now-conscious actors behind him. He had done a masterful job. Like always!

I thought it was all over, but then someone grabbed my shoulder. I looked back to see Carlos. I hated to do it, but I pushed Tom Cruise into him. I just prayed I hadn't ruined Tom's beautiful face. Carlos threw him onto the ground and they began fighting.

I held Randy's hand tight and led the actors over to Biggie. They started chanting, "Kill him! Kill him!" He dashed into the elevator, trying to escape.

Someone fired a shot and Biggie fell to the ground. I looked back to see Kennedy holding a smoking gun.

"He's useless to me now. I'd suggest you say your prayers, Mclintock. You're going to be joining him. Kind of fitting. You two were together for so long in life, you should be together in death." He pointed the gun at me.

Chapter Sixty-Four

I was about to offer up a silent prayer when another man jumped on top of Kennedy. The man punched him, but Kennedy punched back. Then a shot rang out. Both men stopped moving. The other man got up holding his bleeding shoulder.

It was Doctor Feldman. He smiled at me. Then several policemen arrived with the fake Harris in handcuffs.

Thank God it was over.

The good doctor had apparently been working with Kennedy until he realized that I wasn't the guilty one he'd made me out to be. When he told Kennedy he wouldn't work with him anymore, Kennedy had plans to kill him and blame that on me. The doctor escaped and followed Kennedy to the lab. He called the police, but when they didn't arrive in time, he decided to take matters into his own hands.

I thanked the good doctor for his help and he offered me some free sessions.

The next day, I straightened out everything with the police and I was free of all charges. hey let me go with a reprimand about not running away the next time I was arrested even if I was up for an academy award. Reluctantly, I agreed.

I got Shorty out of jail and the guys and I have kept in touch. Of course, Randy thanked me for saving her and so did Edith, who moved in with her permanently. But a week later, when my apartment was being renovated and I showed up at their front door with my suitcase, and my Michael Caine DVD's, oddly enough, they didn't seem that excited to see me. Still, they did let me stay, although, Randy and Edith had lots of rules.

I look forward to some good times with my compadres.

I'm back working on the phones for Lowenthal who doesn't seem to have any more appreciation for my skills. My new agent, Laura, has been trying to get me another audition with the Leaside Reparatory Theatre, but no luck as yet. Next week, I have a part in a TV show where I play a dead man who rolls down a hill.

THE END

ABOUT THE AUTHOR

Steve Shrott's mystery short stories have been published in numerous print magazines and e-zines. His work has appeared in ten anthologies—two from Sisters-in-Crime (*The Whole She-Bang,* and *Fishnets)*. He was a winner in "The Joe Konrath Short Story Contest"(2006). His comedy material has been used by well-known performers of stage and screen (including Joan Rivers and Phyllis Diller) and he has written a book on how to create humor. As well, he teaches humor writing at various real world and cyber schools (such as "Savvy Authors" and "Romance Writers of America"). Some of the jokes he wrote for Phyllis Diller are featured in an article about her in the March 2007 issue of *The Smithsonian Magazine.*